LAGENIENSIS

Legend lays of Ireland

LAGENIENSIS

Legend lays of Ireland

ISBN/EAN: 9783741193125

Manufactured in Europe, USA, Canada, Australia, Japa

Cover: Foto ©Andreas Hilbeck / pixelio.de

Manufactured and distributed by brebook publishing software
(www.brebook.com)

LAGENIENSIS

Legend lays of Ireland

LEGEND LAYS

OF

IRELAND.

BY

LAGENIENSIS.

"To search with mother-love the gifts
Our land can boast—
Soft Erna's isles, Neagh's wooded slopes,
Clare's iron coast ;
Kildare, whose legends grey our bosoms stir
With fay and ghost ;
Grey Mourne, grim Antrim, purple Glenmalur—
Lene's fairy host ;
With raids to many a foreign land to learn to love dear Ireland most."

CHARLES GAVAN DUFFY.

DUBLIN :
JOHN MULLANY, 1 PARLIAMENT-STREET.
1870.

Dedication

TO

WILLIAM JOHN FITZPATRICK, ESQ., J.P.,

KILMACUD MANOR, STILLORGAN.

~~~~~~~~~~~~~~

I.

WHERE'ER in after time our lot be cast,
  While flitting years convey their solemn warning,
Fast bonds of life close link us to the past,
  Though fade from view bright beams of youth's gay
    morning.
  Yet through a prism of thought, false mirage scorning,
Fair imaged tints dispel our sorrows, fears ;
  Mind's magic impress, still each sphere adorning,
Lightens in age the eye bedimmed with tears,
And oft man's drooping heart to noblest progress cheers.

II.

Though bounding o'er an ocean, far away,
    Gazing from steeps, not less sublimely grand,
Wondering, I've paused upon my pilgrim way,
    Apart from sights and shores of Fatherland ;
    In bustling city-halls, by ship-lined strand,
I've heard the stranger's voice of welcome greet :
    Still 'mid their pleasures oft a social band
Would turn perforce t' indulge some converse sweet,
On homes and friends, we lov'd, in former days to meet.

III.

Full many an hour, in errant, pensive mood,
    Pleased with ideas born of earlier scenes,
I've conjured visions by lone stream and wood,
    No human sound disturbed those waking dreams,
    Shadowing so vaguely forms for mental themes.
Our Isle of beauty, famed in tale and song,
    Bless'd me exiled, with strange or distant gleams
Of its weird realms : To thee at length belong
Those legends, cull'd betimes, verse-wreathed far fields
    among—

IV.

To thee, so dear—whose merit firm enthrals—
  Pure, generous, cordial, trusted as a friend,
Whose genial virtues please, whose lore forestalls
  The tone of Irish hearts.   If thou'lt unbend
  From worthier subjects drawn, few moments lend,
And jocund join the glittering fairy train,
  Through some fair Island scenes, that haply blend
Their own lov'd charms, to gloss the storied strain,
Opening new vistas wide, through Fancy's rich domain.

V.

By thine own fireside placed, with one whose gifts
  Of mind and person bless and grace thy home,
When fantasy hath scope, and hand uplifts
  Those leaves so lightly near thy pathway strown,
  Her radiant eye, through mystic realms unknown,
Some glimpse might take few spell-bound hours to while:
  Midst the young household circle, round both grown,
May health and peace long years of life beguile,
And blissful fortune crown each day with favouring smile.
                                        LAGENIENSIS.

CONTENTS.

PREFACE.

POPULAR superstitions derive their origin from remote
periods and various motive causes. They usually result from disordered intellect, imperfect knowledge
and neglected education. However widely extended
those absurd and irreligious notions may have been,
and notwithstanding well-defined lines of distinction,
prevailing in the habits, customs, and usages amongst
different races, classes and creeds, inhabiting our globe,
almost universal belief in irrational supernatural illusions can be assigned to obvious natural causes.
Sacred Scripture and even profane history are
frequently interspersed with accounts of ancient
errors and idolatry, the ever fruitful parents of popular delusion and impiety. Divine Revelation
furnishes irrefragable authority, regarding the origin
of evil, whilst even human experience affords con-
clusive evidence and convincing argument proving its
destructive influence. The natural and cultivated
powers of man's mind, though capable of exalted illu-
mination, are yet finite. The human understanding
has been clouded, as a consequence of our primal fall.
Scepticism or infidelity may assign other causes to
account for such results; but the force of argument

cannot gainsay these facts nor invalidate convincing testimony, establishing inferences drawn from Reason and Revelation.

However differing in details and degree, the usual tenacity of erroneous impressions seems to have established a sort of almost universal domination over all nations. The creed of superstition is nearly similar amongst the people of most countries. Ordinary results of inquiry furnish a coherence of deduction, and a link of connexion, resembling in some degree investigations regarding comparative Philology and the generalizing of extensive historical or scientific researches. In the infancy of science, mystery settled over undiscovered secrets of natural phenomena. Conjectural reveries required slight mental discipline, whilst imagination easily winged her flight to conclusions, little consonant with rational principles. The mind, essentially active, will undoubtedly form more or less inadequately some general idea of natural and inexplicable objects, coming within the range of observation.

In preparing the present little work for publication, the writer felt desirous of correcting or counteracting, to a certain extent, many false statements or inferences made by writers, in reference to various religious practices and to prevailing opinions of a great majority amongst the Irish people. Such misrepresentation is partly owing to incorrect information regarding points of religious dogma, and to a want of appreciating the exact purport of expressions or practices, which spring from undefined but well understood material distinctions between their authoritative Faith and merely fluctuating national traditions or vague mythological opinions. The innermost feelings or sentiments and imagery of language, prevailing amongst our Catholic peasantry in Ireland, cannot be thoroughly known by strangers to their habits of thought, and who ought not expect to become the depositories of secrets, tending to expose those who might unreservedly communicate them to sarcasm or ridicule, by no means congenial to the self-esteem of a sensitive people. Many of our un-Catholic novelists and tale-writers have drawn largely on their inventive faculties for purposes of embellishment and illustration of our popular legends. Yet no person, well acquainted with the habits, customs, and superstitions of the peasantry, could be at a loss to point out various *mal-apropos* allusions, expressions, or inventions, which appear injudicious and inelegant in our national literature, as those miserable and witless songs or dramas, which once furnished the stage with -caricatures of Irish character, speech and manners.

The Legends of Ireland and Tales illustrating many superstitious notions of our peasantry are usually full of lively fancy, imagery, harmless humour and playful imagination. Popular superstitions are not confined to the Irish, as can easily be proved, by comparing our fairy lore with that of other nations. Even the English, Welsh, and Scotch are much more superstitious than the Irish. Nor are superstitions restricted to the less educated classes in those various countries where they prevail. Even, in cases where education might be supposed to exclude vulgar errors, early prepossessions or associations leave their strange impress on minds of superior intelligence. Vague and undefined fears, the observance of lucky and unlucky days, or omens, or predestined anticipations of future misfortunes, characterize the habits, or feelings, and influence the conduct of persons, moving in the very highest circles of society.

It is rather remarkable, and it serves probably to account, in a great measure, for the natural good humour, gentleness and generous dispositions of the Irish, that our popular mythology has few revolting superstitions or horrible creations of fancy connected with it. Even those fictions of more fearful import and gross conception, linked to the indigenous, sportive and light airy fabrications of our legend mongers, would seem to have been incorporated with brain illusions, derived from foreign sources. The blood-stained spectres and fleshless skeletons of German legends; the terror-inspiring night howls of demons and the monstrous shapes of ogres, giants or perturbed warriors of Scandinavian Sagas; the fearful *denoue-*

ments of revenge and disaster following such apparitions, and freezing the very soul of sensibility with horror; these and kindred subjects rarely intrude on our imaginations, or if introduced, they seem toned to a degree, more in unison with ancient and modern instincts of civilization. Witchcraft, as forming a deeply seated theory among the superstitions of our sister islands, with those monstrous repressive enactments of no very remote legislation and executive severity, does not appear to have prevailed extensively in Ireland, previous to the twelfth century. The practice of placing *changelings* or *weaklings* on a red-hot shovel, to expel the fairy spirit, or of throwing persons into water to discover whether they would sink or swim, or of terrifying the supposed preternatural being with a heated poker or some such instrument, is referable only to that class of judicial trials, which caused suspected persons to walk barefooted over the glowing ploughshare or which kindled the fires of persecution for victims of popular delusion. Well authenticated instances of racking torture and gross cruelty, inflicted on innocent and suffering human beings within these realms, and traceable to gross, revolting superstition, resulting in the death of such afflicted persons, have unfortunately in too many instances stained our criminal jurisprudence and outraged all the finer feelings of humanity, at no very remote period. Happily for the fair fame of our island,

those barbarous incidents rarely occurred within it
nor can decided traces of such humiliating enactmenti
and monstrous usages be discovered among the recordi
of our past history.

It seems rather strange, that so few of our native
writers have sought subjects for thought and expression,
in prose and verse, from the legend lore of Erinn.
Assuredly this is capable of arresting and captivating
imagination and fancy to the highest degree.   However, our earlier Irish poets and romancists, who wrote
in the English language, generally selected other
themes, than such as might be derived from popular
superstitions and national legends.   Although, so far
back, as the reign of Elizabeth, Spenser has some
fanciful images and ideas, characterizing a romantic
period or locality, and scattered through his magic
lines, "ofspring of Elves and Faryes;" yet, do we
look in vain through the poems of Sir John Denham, *
those of the vigorous writer, Dr. Jonathan Swift,† or
his friend Parnell,‡ for corresponding fantasies.   Still
among the Poems of this latter graceful writer, we
find a fairy tale, in the ancient English style, as the
poet informs us.   However its scenes and names may
be Anglicised, Parnell acknowledges, in one of its con-
cluding stanzas, he had learned the subject matter

---

* Born in Dublin, A.D. 1615.

† Born in Hoey's Court, Dublin, A.D. 1667.

‡ Born in Dublin, A.D. 1679.

from an Irish nurse.   Accordingly, Edwin, Edith and
Sir Topaz are transferred to

> " Britain's isle and Arthur's days,
> When midnight fairies danc'd the maze."*

Nor do we discover anything legendary in the Poems
of Samuel Boyse,† of the gifted Oliver Goldsmith,‡ of
John Cunningham,§ or of Matthew West;‖ all of
whom belonged to the eighteenth century.

In a whimsical and predantic collection of poems,¶
published by Samuel Whyte, only one of his lucu-
brations intituled, " The Hone, a Piece of Irish
Mythology," has any affinity with our legendary
literature.   In this particular instance, too, the inventive power, taste or delicacy of the author does not
appear to advantage.   A beautiful English metrical
translation of an Irish Cᴀoᴉɴe, or a Lament for Miss
Mary Bourke by Morian Shehone, will be found in
Barry's *Songs of Ireland*.   It is replete with feeling,
we have no doubt, in the original, which probably belongs to the last century, as in the translation, which

---

* This tale is almost identical with the "Lusmore" of Crofton
Croker.

† Born in Dublin, A.D. 1708.

‡ Born in Pallas, Parish of Forgney, County of Longford, A.D. 1728.

§ Born in Dublin, A.D. 1729.

‖ Poems, &c. on several occasions, by Matthew West, A.M. Curate-
assistant of St. Mary's, Donnybrook, and Chaplain to the Rt. Rev.
Isaac, Lord Bishop of Cork. Dublin : John Exshaw, 86 Dame-st. 4to.

¶ The Shamrock, or Hibernian Cresses.   Dublin, 1772: 4to.

appears to have been versified in the present; and it illustrates a national custom, now nearly obsolete. In Rev. William Hamilton's *Letters concerning the Northern Coast of the County of Antrim,* we have few legends. However, one of these, relating to the Scotch M'Donalds and the Irish M'Quillan, must be noted.† In another, we learn that Fin M'Cool built the Giant's Causeway, to connect the shores of Ireland and Scotland.‡ Some of the Magazines, conducted in Dublin during the last century, have a few references to Irish legend lore; but the information conveyed has little to recommend it of a novel, an authentic or interesting character.

It must ever be regretted, that our illustrious poet, Thomas Moore, had not directed the play of his lively and varied genius towards that inexhaustible mine of wealth, which our Irish traditions must have afforded his bright imaginings. In the *Irish Melodies*, it is true, he has left us a legacy that must be greatly prized by his countrymen; and perhaps all the greater, because his national legendary allusions are so rarely detected. If, instead of seeking so many themes for immortal song in Eastern climes, he had confined the muse to subjects, culled from our Island's history and romance; we cannot doubt, his fame as a poet should

---

* Published in Dublin, 1790. 8vo.

† See Part i. Letter vii.

‡ Part ii. Letter i.

not suffer decrease, while his patriotic services to Ireland must have extended her renown and have rendered his own name even more a household word by Irish firesides.

We have now to deal with the romantic literature of the present age, so far as it is concerned with Irish song and story. The "Life of Thomas Dermody," edited by James Grant Raymond,* is found interspersed with various pieces of original poetry and private correspondence. These serve to exhibit the unexampled precociousness of his genius, before the early death of this intemperate and unfortunate young poet. Rarely, however, does he "the native legends of his land rehearse."

In the early part of this century, his young friend, Miss Owenson—afterwards the brilliant and accomplished Lady Morgan—sent forth in rapid succession her "Lay of an Irish Harp," with her "Wild Irish Girl," "O'Donnell," "Florence Macarthy," "The O'Briens and O'Flaherties," &c. Although this admired authoress produced highly effective tales of national life and manners, spiced with sarcastic and merited attacks on the disorganisation, ascendancy and covert popular discontent, arising from a wretched state of society and oppression prevalent at this period, she has casually alluded—but in a few instances only—to

---

* Published in 2 vols. London, 1806, 8vo.

the legend lore of her native land. The amiable and erudite authoress, Mrs. Henry Tighe of Rosanna, has produced one of the most charming classical and moralistic allegories in our language, in the Spenserian stanza, and she has left rather beautiful fragments of verse.* Here, indeed, we find allusions to Irish scenes, persons and subjects. Yet we detect a total absence of any additions to our popular legendary literature, which the elegant fancy and imagination of the gifted authoress could have invested with peculiar graces of conception and composition.

It may not be generally known, that John D'Alton wrote a metrical romance, in twelve cantos, and entitled, *Dermid*,† which procured him the acquaintance and correspondence of Lord Byron and of Sir Walter Scott. This juvenile yet highly creditable poem contains allusions to many curious customs, usages and superstitions of the Irish and Danes. In the text and notes, such information is found gracefully and pleasingly distributed. We exempt altogether from this brief account all reference to the valuable volumes, which our dear, deceased old friend published, and which so well serve to illustrate Irish local and family history. In the *Fairy Legends and Traditions of the South of Ireland*,‡ T. Crofton

---

* See, Psyche, with other Poems. By the late Mrs. Henry Tighe, London, 1811. 4to.

† Published at London, in 1814, by Longman and Co. 4to.

‡ This highly popular work appeared anonymously for the first

Croker evinces a brilliant, sportive and poetic fancy in his mode of treatment, while he combines singular erudition, in tracing the connexion between our Irish fairy traditions and those current among people living in other countries.   To his charming pages are we indebted for a rich vein of invention and illustration. To him may well be applied the exquisite lines of his own provincial bard Callanan, in the inimitable stanzas descriptive of Gougane Barra.   By tireless industry, enthusiasm and aptitude for the task, it was Crofton Croker, who

"gleaned each grey legend that darkly was sleeping,
When the mist and the rain o'er their beauty was creeping."

In the poetic vein, also, Croker has rendered the fairy romances of " Cormac and Mary" and " The Lord of Dunkerron" into rythmical lines, which evidence his taste and genius.   He had likewise previously described many curious customs and usages of the Irish, in connexion with fairies and supernatural agency, keens and death ceremonies, in the Fifth and Ninth Chapters of an interesting, illustrated work, entitled, *Researches in the South of Ireland.**

---

time, in 1825, and was published in London, by Murray. A second edition, illustrated by Maclise, rapidly followed to supply the exhaustive demand for the first.   Thomas Wright, Esq., a friend of the author, has edited a beautiful and portable 8vo, edition, published by William Tegg, London, in 1862.   It is preceded by a brief Memoir of Crofton Croker.   ·

* Published in London, by Murray, 1824. 4to.

Excepting the " Songs of Deardra," versified from an old Irish manuscript, and recounting the tragic adventures of this heroine and the death of the sons of Usna, in his volume of Poems* Thomas Stott has left us nothing, which serves to illustrate Irish legendary story. In Thomas Furlong's posthumous national poem, *The Doom of Derenzie*, published by Robins of London, much curious information on Irish fairy mythology and popular customs will be found scattered throughout the text and notes. One of the principal characters in this poem is an Irish Fairyman or wizard. The original, from whom he was drawn, is regarded as being a native of Wexford county. He was named Shane Wrue, or, John Roe. The Remains of the Rev. Charles Wolfe, A.B., as edited by the Rev. John A. Russell, M.A.,† present us with nothing fancifully referring to "Faerie lond." In that most interesting work, " Irish Minstrelsy," edited by James Hardiman, we find many bardic remains in the native tongue. These are elegantly rendered into English verse, by such writers as Thomas Furlong, John D'Alton, Edward Lawson, Henry Grattan Curran, Rev. William Hamilton Drummond. In this scarce and valuable work, we have many of Carolan's remains and other ancient relics included. They have been

---

* Published in London, 1825. 8vo.

† See, Ninth Edition, London, 1847. 12mo.

introduced, with a richness of illustration, most creditable to the taste and erudition of Mr. Hardiman.* About this time, likewise, our Irish novelists and poets, John Banim and Gerald Griffin were achieving fame for themselves and their country, by the admirable productions, which issued from the press in London, and which must continue to instruct and amuse unborn generations. The Rev. Cæsar Otway's "Tour in Connaught"† and "Sketches in Ireland,"‡ with many other narratives, contain many a droll legend and story, related in a rollicking and humourous vein, but with improbable circumstances infused, and tending to throw unworthy aspersion on the old religious creed of our countrymen.

The *Dublin Penny Journal* of 1832 to 1836, the *Irish Penny Magazine* of 1833-34, and the *Irish Penny Journal* of 1840-41, contain many racy tales and legends of Ireland, by accomplished native pensmen. Some of the foregoing writers, with others unknown, were facile contributors to the columns of these illustrated miscellanies, the prized *feuilletons* of our school-boy days. Then, poor Edward Walsh placed on record some of Munster's traditional folk-lore. Carleton, likewise, penned that awe-inspiring *romaunt*, "Sir

---

* His work was published in two volumes, by Joseph Robins London, 1831. 8vo.

† Dublin, Wm. Curry Jun. & Co., 1839. 12mo.

‡ Dublin, Wm. Curry Jun. & Co., 1839. 12mo. Second Edition.

Turlough, or the Church-yard Bride." Many another talented contributor obtained insertion for various Irish tales and legends.

From our early reminiscences to the present date, occasional acquaintance with numbers of the *Dublin University Magazine** had introduced to us the now familiar names of several national writers, in connexion with Irish legendary lore. Here have we met with the racy "Kishoge Papers"—the metrical version of Dame Alice Kettle's trial for sorcery and entitled, "The Witch of Kilkenny"—the inimitable Golden Legend and Voyage of St. Brendan, with other metrical contributions, by one of the foremost amongst our modern poets, Denis Florence M'Carthy. The "Songs of the Superstitions of Ireland," with several legendary ballads,† issuing from the pen of the facetious Samuel Lover; those beautifully picturesque and historic narratives, "Hibernian Nights' Entertainments," by Samuel Ferguson; the anonymous "Legends and Tales of the Queen's County Peasantry," true to life and redolent of genius, which are now known as the contributions of an humble national schoolmaster, John Keegan; many beautiful and anonymous metrical productions of the gifted James Clarence Mangan, and all of which

---

* First issued, January, 1833, and continued to the present time.

† These have been since published in a collective form by Chapman and Hall, London.

have not been as yet published in book shape; those spirit-stirring Orange slogans of Lieutenant-Colonel Blacker,* and those equally intensified true-blue lines of Miss E. M. Hamilton; William Carleton's exaggerated "Traits and Stories of the Irish Peasantry," with a visible improvement in etching and colouring national life and character, as he advanced; various graceful and descriptive papers on "Irish Rivers," by J. Roderick O'Flanagan; these, and various other talented contributions, gave a permanent interest and popularity to our stock of Island Legends. Editorial and frenzied attacks on Daniel O'Connell, doubting his claims to be considered a distinguished Irishman, because of his advocating Reform, Abolition of Tithes and Repeal of the Union; lashing Thomas Moore for his Fudges in England; abusing Lover for his Rory O'Moore, as being dangerously national; ungallantly denouncing Miss Harriet Martineau for being liberal; dealing unmeasured strokes on the Whig Archbishop Wheatly, Lord Mulgrave and the Rev. Sydney Smith; while proclaiming the mountebank, Rev. Mortimer O'Sullivan a political and religious Soloman; we may now indulge some pleasantry over reversed judgments, and the less intellectual pages of this fine serial. Such distinguished *litterateurs* or *femmes savantes* as Mrs. Hemans, Rev. Cæsar Otway, William Allingham, Anna

---

* He often writes under the signature of Fitz-Stewart, Bannside.

Maria Hall, Rev. James Wills,* John Anster, LL.D.,
Charles Lever, Maxwell, William R. Wilde, with
"Speranza," Aubrey de Vere, Jonathan Freke Slingsby
(John Francis Waller, LL.D.), T. Irwin, John Ffraser
and John Fisher Murray were found pleasantly carica-
turing or truthfully illustrating some peculiar features
of Irish life, character or scenery.† These writers,
with a kindly elasticity of spirit, rose above the billows
of party feeling, which then seethed and effervesced.
They lent to Irish national literature those strokes of
wit and genius, which must ever serve to perpetuate
their memories in popular estimation.

---

* Some elegant Dramatic Sketches and other Poems of this writer
were published in Dublin, A.D. 1847, in 8vo. The Disembodied and
other Poems were issued in 12mo by the same author.

† Some of the following metrical Legends also appeared in the
Dublin University Magazine. Indeed, it may be said, that one of
them made its *debut* a second time, with some change of phraseology,
and under the following circumstances. About the year 1849, while
residing in a distant country, the "Legend of Loughrea," with notes
attached, had been sent to a gentleman in Dublin. It would seem,
that the *Dublin University Maga ine* editor got possession of this
fragment, and gave it insertion in the xxxvii. vol. at p. 676. It is
there acknowledged as bearing a foreign postage mark. At a subsequent period, the lines in question, with notes somewhat different,
were offered to and accepted by a successor in the editorial chair. It
is only right to observe, however, that neither this gentleman nor the
author had been cognizant of the fact relating to a first insertion,
when the Legend obtained a second and misplaced introduction to the
pages of our national Magazine.

It must suffice to state, that about the year 1842, Mr. and Mrs. Hall's beautifully illustrated work, *Ireland : its Scenery, Character, &c.*, first appeared. It is richly studded with legends and highly dramatic strokes of graphic national delineation. Indeed, it must almost prove an impossible task to enumerate the various short-lived Irish periodicals, since published in this country, with the names and productions of writers, who have merited honourable mention connected with this peculiar subject. Although Davis certainly composed many noble historic and soul-stirring ballads, he has not at all turned his powers of versification to the less exciting subject of mere legendary romance. However, we need only refer to the *Ballads of Ireland*, collected and edited by Edward Hayes, for confirmation of the fact, that our legendary literature has been cultivated with great taste and genius by native writers. Among the more modern of our poets and publicists, Richard D. Joyce, Patrick Kennedy, Hercules Ellis, T. D. Sullivan, J. F. O'Donnel, and that modest son of genius, the anonymous author of *The Monks of Kilcrea*, deserve highly honourable record. It is to be hoped they will frequently recur for inspiration to the clear fount of Irish lore. That the subjects it presents can ever be exhausted is simply impossible ; while the sooner it is gleaned and garnered, whether in verse or prose, the better chance must exist for the preservation of many interesting popular traditions.

An attempt at instructing the lower orders of people through the medium of their superstitions has been advocated, as one of the most attractive and successful methods for imparting information, while combining knowledge with amusement. It is certain, that many foolish and even barbarous superstitions, habits or customs have often been eradicated by delicate sarcasm and effective publicity. Rooted prejudices and relics of by-gone absurd usages or superstitions gradually give place to the force of enlightened public opinion and advancing civilization.

Among the earliest impressions made on youthful minds, the wanderings of our imaginative faculties are sure to leave their impress, before judgment can assert the exercise of her corrective powers. To visit the light-hearted peasant's cabin or to form one of its social circle during long winter evenings is popularly known as *courdheaghing*. How agreeable to our youthful fancies, the harmless and pleasant jokes of young and old, at these humble cheerful *re-unions!* How many weird tales of goblin and fairy were told, and to auditors perdisposed for receiving most wonderful descriptions and adventures with reverential assent! How many romantic and long-drawn narratives were spun out through the night by some professional story-teller, and which were only varied by the rustic ballad, containing an almost interminable quantity of verses! How often has not the Irish peasant's child fallen asleep, through downright tension of eager desire to follow the story-teller to his *denouement* of a giant's mishap and a successful exit of adventure to the youngest son of some imaginary king and queen! The subject matter for such tales beguiled the hours of rest and often of field labour, among our humble classes. Similar narratives in prose and verse once engaged the attention of " high-born ladye" and belted chieftain, in the time-honoured keep or baronial hall, many ages past: nor can we doubt but this practice of story-telling descended from the old castle and bard or *shanachie*, to the modern cabin and wandering *bocagh* or *shuler*, who received a bed, bit and sup, "for God's sake," from the humble but generous peasant, and whose arrival was welcomed all the more, by parent and child, when naturally though rudely gifted with " sweet wit and good invention," like the Irish bards of whom Spenser writes. These tales, however, were only intended to while away time agreeably, without making any great demands on the cottier's credulity. Is it therefore wonderful, that early associations and training should accustom the peasant, from his very childhood, to re-ceive romantic impressions and to cultivate ideality, thinking or talking, asleep or waking? Hence, like-wise, we can scarcely feel surprised, that the number of Irish tales and legends is so varied and inex-haustible.

The following metrical productions have been composed in different places, and during some disengaged moments, not occupied by more pressing employments or serious duties. They range over a period of nearly the last thirty years. Some of those have already appeared in periodicals; but most of them are now issued for the first time; while in their present collected form, they have undergone considerable correction and revision. They are designed to preserve some old traditions, popular notions, local legends, historic facts and scenic delineations of Ireland; still, they only comprise very few selections from a number of similar subjects, quite as interesting, yet hitherto unknown, to the reading public.

Dublin, February, 1870.

LEGEND LAYS OF IRELAND.

No. I.

A Legend of Killarney.

THE SILVER-HOOFED STEED OF O'DONOGHUE.

O! saw you the spectre this moon-paling night,
How stately he glides, on a charger of white,
Where the large wavy circles recedingly break,
As the silver hoof pitches a foam o'er the lake. [1]

'Tis the Chief of the Glens, whose untiring career
Is viewed on the loveliest morn of the year,
With his courtiers of air, and his fays of the rath,
Strewing garlands and flowers round his watery path.

And as legends relate, the same sight shall be seen
When the May month comes round, with its young buds
        of green;
When the violets spring in the thorn-tangled dales,
And the hare-bells and primroses blossom the vales.

And the cliffs of Glenane shall their echoes prolong, [2]
That arise from the revels and sweet elfin song;
The course be unchequered and flowing the rein,
Till the steed his bright plates shall have worn on Lane.

Then the currach [3] and boatman shall rock on the flow
Of those waves that roll over a palace below;
And the minstrel of air shall attune the lyre's strings
To those strains he once sung at the banquet of kings.

Then the snowy arbutus shall blossom that brow
Where the plume-waving helmet encircles it now;
And those dances, the fairy band thoughtlessly whirls
On the crest of the lake, shall be tripped on its pearls. [4]

No more shall O'Donoghue [5] visit the steeps
That were guarded by grey, frowning, ancestral keeps:
No more shall the May morn dawning discover
The airy career of the water-sprite rover.

Long, long, shall he revel in fairy halls bright,
Nor once ply a spur through the motionless night,
Nor dash with his courser, nor sport with his train, .
On the blue, mirrored surface of reek-crested Lane.

NOTES.

[1] Amongst the many accounts current of O'Donoghue, the fabled Chieftain of the Lakes, is that of his charger having the hoofs shod with silver plates. When the latter become entirely worn by their action on wave and shore, as the boatmen believe or assert, the chieftain, with his steed and attendants, will for ever disappear from mortal vision.

[2] The most celebrated echoes of Killarney are produced from the wooded steeps of Glenane. The echo at the precipitous cliff called the *Eagle's Nest* has a most unearthly and astonishing effect, when awakened by a concert of boatmen's bugles. It would seem, as if numbers of invisible instrumental performers were repeating from a spirit world the notes already produced, and as if those sounds were

resumed, after they had at first died away, by musicians stationed far off amongst the adjacent mountains. That beautiful air, *The Last Rose of Summer*, is a favorite melody of the boatmen, who place themselves at a mound opposite the *Eagle's Nest*, and on the right bank of that duct of water, called the *Long Range*. Tourists are usually placed in their boats, drawn up close to the bank, and in such a situation, as to lose sight of the instrumentalists. It would be impossible to convey an adequate impression to the mind of the reader, as it would be equally improbable ever to forget the sensation produced on the mind of the writer, in connexion with a performance of the exquisite air already alluded to, by a pair of excellent buglers, on occasion of a visit to the justly celebrated Lakes of Killarney. There is also a fine echo awakened from Ross Castle and Island, on the Lower Lake.

[3] Such was the name given to a boat used by the primitive inhabitants of Ireland. It was constructed of wicker-work, covered with the hides of animals. It is needless to premise, that the currach has long since disappeared from the waters of Killarney, having been replaced by the modern well-appointed pleasure-boat, so generally approved by tourists and visitors.

[4] The Lakes of Killarney are known to abound in beautiful pearls. They are found in great numbers, especially in the River Laune, which conducts the waters of Lough Lane towards Dingle Bay, and thence to the ocean. It would appear, that these romantic lakes were celebrated for their pearls even in days remote. Amongst the O'Longan MSS. (Vol. xxii. p. 326) of the Royal Irish Academy, there is an anonymous Poem on the Death of Feidhlimidh, the son of Crimhthann, king of Munster, and disputed monarch of Ireland, who died in the year 822. The poet gives an interesting account of a royal visit paid by Felim to his reluctant subjects of Connaught, Ulster and Leinster. This visit lasted three years, during which time the monarch and his immense host of followers lived at free quarters, in the districts through which they passed. The minor tributes of the king are mentioned in this poem, and among them we find the following very curious items : viz. Scarlet dying-stuff, from Bearra; Wheat, from Cualann in Wicklow ; Apples, from Leithghlinn; Dulisk, from

the Skelligs, in Kerry; *Pearls, from Loch Lein or Killarney*; Razor-fish, from Whiddy Island; Salt, from Ard Ladhrann, County of Waterford; Saddle skins, from Tralee; Deal or Fir Wands, from Offaly; Cuarans or raw-hide shoes, from Raighne, in the same district; Honey, from Doire Modomnoc, which the late Professor Eugene O'Curry believes to have been in the south of Ossory.   The poem in question is a very scarce tract.

[5] This mythic personage is the constant subject of various wild and incredible legends, amongst the Killarney boatmen and guides. The stories of more recent invention usually manifest less imagination and romantic incident, than others of an earlier date.   The Chieftain of the Lakes is renowned in song as in story.   One of Moore's lightest and most airy melodies has reference to this phantom, whose origin we cannot trace to any accredited historic source.   A poem in seven cantos, by Miss Hannah Maria Bourke, and entitled, *O'Donoghue, Prince of Killarney*, is rather an indifferent production as a poetic effort, although preserving various interesting conceptions and illus trations of the apparition.

No. II.

A Legend of Benevenugh.

THE CAVERN FAIRY COURT.

On the dark northern coast, o'er waves of blue,
  And towering as a giant guard of ocean,
Thy heathered cliffs arise, Benevenugh, [1]
  Proud 'gainst the rushing tempest's wild commotion ;
Proud 'gainst the fierce tornado gusts, that strew
  With angry foam the billows' rapid motion.
And far within thy hollow womb diverge
Caves that re-echo to the rolling surge.

Of old, thy brow was gloomy : and to-day,
  So awful and so savage is thy form,
That rustic chroniclers will trembling say
  Unearthly sounds are heard above the storm,
And much desire to shun thee, as they stray
  Unwillingly before the rise of morn ;
When dark imagination pictures o'er
The visioned scenes and treasured tales of yore.

The fairy Evenue, [2] within thy caves,
  Sways sprites that cower in his dark dominions ;
Hence sallies out, when midnight tempest raves,
  With power to sail about on airy pinions,
When wintry gusts whirl on the withered leaves [8]
  His elfin courtiers round and tiny minions.
The rocking seaman hears with pale affright
Those gathering sounds, loud echoing through the night.

What dreadful deeds, that shun the light, performed
   Within those windings, mortals durst not scan.
The sense of hearing distantly informed
   The terror-stricken, pilgrim-faring man,
Till once a blithesome youth the danger scorned,
   And entering tremblingly his search began :
Whilst tottering through the yawning depths, rock-bound,
The sparry arches ring his footfalls round.

Yet, soon the rocks to other echoes woke ;
   A sound of minstrelsy, in vigorous strains,
As if from distant bagpipe fitful broke,
   Like moans that start, when terror rules the dreams
Of midnight sleepers : and the rocks evoke
   A shrilly, droning melody, that wanes
Anon to stillness : then, it rends the ear,
With swellings on the midnight, wild and clear.

A light gleamed far within the deep recess,
   That burst with dazzling lustre o'er the scene ;
Unearthly nymphs the pattering footsteps press,
   With swains grotesque, on velvet sward of green.
And undiminished seem'd the mirth—nor less
   The chandeliers spread o'er their brilliant sheen
For hours that passed, whilst midnight revels rung,
And gazed the youth on sports, that ever please the
    young.

While seated on a throne, the rest above,
   With hoary locks and beard, their Evenue [4]
Bent o'er the groups with twinkling glance of love,
   That ever and anon more placid grew.

But whilst the ceaseless footsteps circling move,
  A SNEEZE [5] escaped the mortal screened from
    view.
Then ceased the music's strain, the lights grew dim,
And bellowing sounds the rocks repeat within.

Soon turned our rash adventurer to flight,
  With hostile echoes gathering on his rear ;
Nor guide he found, in ushering him to light,
  Whilst trembling limbs betrayed his sense of fear,
And doubly dark within those caves was night.
  But crystal spars, their glimmering light to steer
Lent his uncertain path : the crannies round
Reverberate a clanging, vengeful sound.

It seemed, as if an earthquake for egress
  Were struggling from the rock-surrounded caves ;
As if the winds ploughed up with groaning stress
  The lowest depths of ocean's furrowed waves,
And thunder growled, along the vaults, where press
  Pursuers and pursued.   Their distance leaves
Fast fading hope.   By chance, a glimmering ray
Conducts the mortal safe to hail the dawn of day.

NOTES.

[1] Benevenugh, or Benyevenagh, is a mountain in the county of
Londonderry, and it rises majestically about 1,260 feet above the level
of Lough Foyle. The mountain is of basaltic formation, and from its
summit, in clear weather, commands a most extended range of prospect,
including the celebrated island of Iona, and some of the Western Isles
of Scotland. The tidal waters of Lough Foyle lave the base of Benye-

venagh; and on its precipitous heights over the ocean, eagles are known to breed, whilst flocks of curlews, seagulls and other marine birds hover continually round its sides. The varied botanic productions of this mountain have been long celebrated for their medicinal qualities: the wild flowers that adorn its breast attract swarms of bees in the summer season, and impart a delicious flavour to the honey, procured in the neighbourhood. Over an hundred years ago, the last wolf known to exist in Ulster was started upon Benyevenagh and killed in the woods near Dungiven. In legendary and historic lore, the traditions of the adjoining districts are highly interesting. A mountain in Scotland, mentioned in the opening canto of the " Lady of the Lake," bears a name nearly corresponding in pronunciation with that of our Ultonian highland. It is a double-coned, irregular rocky summit, towering magnificently over a romantic copsed headland and bend, breasting the blue waters of Lough Katrine. It looms with uncommon grandeur on the gaze of the enraptured tourist. Sir Walter Scott sings of

> " The pine-trees blue
> On the bold cliffs of Benvenue."

A considerable portion of Benyevenagh is cultivated and finely wooded, whilst the greater part presents an aspect of bold outline and rugged grandeur.

[2] Evenue, an Anglicised form of Aibhne, is still a common name amongst the O'Kanes of Londonderry. Aibhne was also a favourite Christian name with the former chiefs of this clan, as we can easily ascertain by referring to the ancient annals of Ireland.

[3] It is believed, that the Fairies move from one rath to another, when those eddying winds converge, which raise spiral columns of dust, straws or decaying vegetable matter. Such appearances are denominated *Shee-geehy* or " Fairy blasts," by the peasantry; and to propitiate the invisible elves, it is customary to exclaim, " God speed ye, gentlemen !"

> " When the *Shee-geehy* rolls its boding cloud,
> And arrows unseen in vengeance fly,"

it is always deemed prudent to avoid the direct course, in which the *Slua-shee* or " Fairy host" advances.

[4] Local traditions and its very nomenclature seem to connect Benevenugh with the imaginary being here mentioned; yet, I am not sufficiently versed in folk-lore mythology to elucidate further the history of this tutelary genius and his subordinate spirits. However, it should be known, that Aibhne or Evenue gave name to the ancient territory of Oireacht-Ui Cathain, situated between Lough Foyle and the river Bann, in the county of Londonderry. From this chief, who flourished A.D. 1432, was derived the tribe-name Oireacht-Aibhne, by which the chief families of the O'Kanes were designated. He was the progenitor of nearly all the subsequent chiefs belonging to this family.

[5] The slightest noise or exclamation from a human being is sure to reveal his presence, whenever he intrudes on elfin sports and revels. In this particular, as in a variety of other instances, there is a striking analogy between Irish and Scottish fairy mythology. This resemblance is even more apparent in the legends of the province of Ulster. A *dénouement* somewhat similar to that recorded in the present instance occurred in Burns' tale of " Tam o' Shanter;" for no sooner had the hero cried out,

> "' Weel done, Cutty sark !'
> Than in an instant all was dark:
> And scarcely had he Maggie rallied,
> When out the hellish legion sallied."

Sneezing is supposed to be attributable to fairy influences, and hence it is customary to invoke a benediction, immediately after its occurrence. The Irish peasant usually exclaims, " God bless us !" when oppressed with a fit of sternutation; and " God bless you !" is the expected response from the bystanders, who may happen to be present. If the faries can make a person sneeze three times, without any one saying " God bless you," they have it in their power to abduct a person sneezing to their habitations. This fit of sneezing is usually effected by the fairies tickling the mortal's nose with a *traneen* or a blade of barley. " God bless us," after sneezing, was a common expression in the East, and a singular story regarding the origin of this custom will be found in the "Talmud." In that languid state, which superinduces the habit of yawning, a sign of crossing the open mouth with the thumb prevails; but I have not been able to discover the exact purport of such practice. It would seem, that the Pagans regarded sneezing as ominous, and as connected with divination or magic practices. These omens were reprobated and prohibited by various decrees of continental councils and synods, during the earlier ages of Christianity. St. Eligius or Eloy, who became bishop of Noyon, towards the middle of the seventh century, cautions his people against superstitious observations, derived from sneezing; but he recommends them to sign themselves, in the name of Christ, as a remedy or substitute for such unhallowed magic arts. From an ancient poem, quoted in the Irish Version of the *Historia Britonum* of Nennius, it would appear, that before the departure of the Cruithnians or Picts from Ireland to Scotland, they left six druids behind them. Amongst other omens, necromancy and observations, regarding the changes of weather, lucky times and noting the voices of birds, which were peculiar to the practices of druidism and idolatry, these haruspices were remarkable for the honouring or regard bestowed on *a sneezing*, designated by the Irish word, ṁeḋ or ṡṁiaḋ.

No. III.

A Legend of Ormond Castle.

THE BODING RAVEN.

" The cawing rook shall build her nest on Ormond Castle's
pinnacle, [1]
Ere Irish blood shall flow from bands divided and inimical :
Twelve moons shall fill their orbs before fulfilment of that
omen, [2]
And then those parted bands shall meet, in battle-fields, as
foemen."

So ran the Seer's prediction, and the peasant long had
sought her,
The messenger of discord, and the harbinger of slaughter ;
When *Ninety-seven* brought the sign of death and desolation,
And *Ninety-eight* conviction spread, around a mourning nation. [3]

NOTES.

[1] The situation of Ormond Castle, on the banks of the river
Nore, and adjoining the city of Kilkenny, is exceedingly picturesque ;
the fine old feudal mansion has many historic reminiscences connected with its time-honoured walls. The interior contains several
beautiful priceless works of art, and the *Evidence Chamber* abounds in
manuscript materials of great archæological value to the genealogist
and antiquary. The late lamented Marquess of Ormond intended to
publish many of these memorials, which would serve to illustrate the

actions of his distinguished progenitors and some of the most remarkable events in the general history of Ireland. It is to be hoped, that
this intention, frustrated by his untimely death, will yet be realized ;
and it is rumoured, in literary circles, that one of our most accomplished antiquarians, Rev. James Graves, will shortly bring those valuable relics to light, under the auspices of government.

[2] The classic reader will recollect the possibility of tracing this
Irish superstition to a Pagan origin. In the first of Virgil's Eclogues,
the unhappy shepherd Meliboeus also complains :

> " Sæpe malum hoc nobis, si mens non læva fuisset,
> De cœlo tactas memini prædicere quercus.
> Sæpe sinistra cava prædixit ab ilice cornix."

It is considered an omen of evil import to behold a crow or raven, as
the first object seen in the morning. Should it be observed hovering
over or settled on a house, one of the inmates, it is supposed, will
shortly die, or some other great calamity must inevitably befall the
family in possession.

[3] It is stated by different inhabitants of the " fair citie" of Kilkenny, an old prophecy had decreed, that when a rook should build
her nest on the highest turret of Ormond Castle, the following year
was to be characterized by a civil war throughout Ireland. The curious
incident predicted is said to have taken place in the year 1797 ; and a
recollection of the words of this prophecy, as also the singularity of the
circumstance itself, attracted the regards of the peasantry, who flocked
from even distant parts of our Island, to witness the baneful prog-
nostic. The disastrous Rebellion of 1798 and its results are too well
known, in connexion with the general history of this country, and
were supposed to have had a necessary connexion, with this prophetic
indication of the preceding year.

No. IV.

A Legend of Lough Rea.

THE DEATH-SIGN.

WOE to the land! for the warning is given,
 Through the mist of the lake, at the gloaming of day;
And dimly disclosed, through the curtain of even,
 The death-sign is seen from the shores of Lough Rea. [1]

Youth of the land! be the white garland dresses
 Prepared for the grave-yard procession's array: [2]
For the wild breeze shall sweep o'er the snowy wand-
 tresses [3]
 That wave on thy funeral barrows, Lough Rea.

Death to the land! and a death-stroke entailing,
 On the homestead deserted the shriek of dismay;
The light laugh of mirth shall be changed into wailing,
 The living shall weep for the dead of Lough Rea.

NOTES.

[1] The picturesque lake, bearing this name, and situated in the county of Galway, is bounded on the south and east with verdant hills. Three beautiful islets crown its waters. It is said that once in seven years a black coffin may be seen on the waters of Lough Rea, and this apparition is called *the sign*, by the inhabitants of the surrounding country. It is usually thought to herald the approach of pestilence and mortality; whilst the people remark, that almost immediately after

its appearance, great numbers of persons from this neighbourhood are consigned to the tomb.

[2] It was customary, in many parts of Ireland, on the death of unmarried persons, beloved and respected for their virtues, to decorate a long staff with bowed projections on the sides—the wood-work being concealed by fringes of white calico, linen or paper, overlaid in regular ranges. A pair of white paper gloves fell pendant from the hoops. This was properly called *the garland*. A cross was prepared in like manner, together with twelve small and slender sally wands peeled. The tips of the latter, and the projections of the former, were for the most part looped with knots of pink ribbon. The garland-bearer went foremost in the funeral procession, and immediately preceding the coffin: twelve young persons followed two and two, whilst the cross-bearer brought up the rear. If the deceased happened to be a maiden, the processionists were also unmarried females, clothed in white dresses. If the deceased were a young man, the garland, wands and cross were borne by unmarried persons of the same sex. Having arrived at the grave, the garland-bearer stood at the head, the cross-bearer at the foot, the wand-bearers ranging themselves, six on each side. After the last sod had been laid over the deceased, all the bearers stuck down their frail memorials in the earth, according to the order in which they were placed. In some parts of the country the *garland* and its appendages were set up, over the middle of the grave. There these frail mementoes remained, until blown down by the wind.

[3] The French, and perhaps other continental people, have a custom of dressing the graves of their deceased friends with flowers and lighted tapers, on certain festivals. In the large cemetery, near the city of New Orleans, the inhabitants usually observed this practice on All Souls' Day. It would seem, that a practice prevails, in some church-yards adjoining the city of Kilkenny, whereby the graves of deceased relatives are denuded of their green swards, and carefully sanded over by the peasantry, on the festival days of the parish patrons. The sand of finest quality is always selected for such purposes; and it is often brought from a considerable distance—a rivalry actuating those, who consider their labours destined to manifest suitable affection and respect towards the memory of the dead.

No. V.

A Legend of Cullenagh.

THE FAIRY HURLERS.

THE Currach [1] meadows ring with hoot
Of creaking rail and water-coot,
The shrilly pipings of the quail
And bittern's lengthened, mournful wail
   Resound from tufts of blossomed broom ;
Whilst to Cremorgan's woods [2] repair
The cawing rooks through middle air,
   Where myriads seek their leafy home.
The owlet, from his cryptic cell
   In Ballyknocken's castle walls, [3]
Grates his harsh, discordant yell
   As evening's sun descending falls,
Ere he sinks down o'er Cashel's hill [4]
   And closes on the parting day,
Leaving the landscape lone and still,
   Casting a bright vermilion ray,
   On those dismantled walls of gray.
The hurrying clouds were sailing past,
   Stained with a fringe of rosy light,
As the sun lingering looked his last
   And parted from the painless sight :
The valleys, hills, and moors receive
The sombre tints of fading eve.

In early days, I've ranged alone
Amid those scenes, so haply known,

Or from the casement viewed rich floods
Of sun-set brilliance crown the woods.
I've marked the peat-moss shagged with broom
Stretch out its waste, and dun Slieve Bloom
Like vapour on th' horizon float,
Whilst vocal woodlands chime each note ;
And blithely would the mavis sing
From budding hedge, though flowering Spring :
With Summer's robes on distant lines
O'er birchen groves and tasseled pines,
I've scanned each phase with raptured eye,
Whilst sunrise flushed the orient sky,
From dewy morn, through torrid noon,
To evening-tide's uprising moon :
Through Autumn, when the reaper shears
His yielding rows of sun-brown'd ears,
Whilst jocund laugh from binder's train
Inspires with mirth the bending swain.
When gathering clouds, their copious grist
Discharged in gusts of murky mist,
With chilling floods o'er mead and plain,
Through Winter's wild and cheerless reign.
Freed from the irksome task and rule
That linked each prosy hour to school,
While sped these days in careless prime
I took few notes of passing time,
When listening to the wildering trail
Of incident through magic tale,
But well I conned such wond'rous lore
As rustics taught in times of yore.
The light thus gleaned might well impinge

On canvass every rainbow tinge,
Might shoot fair rays to latest age
In wildest scenes of fiction's page,
Or plume imagination's wing
With themes that minstrels dream or sing.

Midsummer held her reign in June,
When snowy hawthorn blossoms bloom
   And fragrant air perfumes the weather :
Night wore on that stilly noon,
When rose the round and cloudless moon,
   O'er Cullenagh's dark mountain heather. [5]
Kilvahan, [6] where the village dead
Rest in their cold sepulchral bed,
Has ceased loud echoes to repeat
Of milkmaid's song and lambkin's bleat.
The fleecy flocks now rest among
Tall, sheltering slabs, that crown each tomb.
The lingering morn her rise delayed,
Sliabh Dubh [7] had cast a sombre shade,
   Upon the Middle Mountain [8] drawn,
Till climbing high above his head
The moon her mellowed radiance spread,
   E'en on the smooth crest of Sliabh Bawn. [9]
The mountain water of the Foyle, [10]
   Pent within its barrier hold,
With breasted wavelets, that recoil
   And seem like a plain of molten gold.
But flashing clear with pearly brightness,
   The rushing streams of silv'ry fountains,

Rivalling new fallen snow in whiteness,
　And leaping down the shelving mountains,
In wild commotion hoarsely brawl
O'er many a glen and waterfall.
The birds of song their feathered breasts
Recline in shaded, downy nests;
No more their strains awake the dales,
The noiseless hills and slumbering vales.
· The yellow furze, the stunted thorn,
The verdant meads, the ripening corn,
The cots around gleam in her light,
As the moon brings the middle night.

On such a night—at such an hour—
　Young Connor's steps, as home he hied,
Disturbed by some delirious power,
　Moved measureless from side to side;
The dust-drawn circles, tangents, sines,
And aught save rectilinear lines,
Gave mathematic demonstrations
Of awkward moves and dubious stations.
His eyes saw not, or saw things double,
　His reeling brain, from time to time,
Dismissing thoughts of care and trouble,
　Launched forth upon the true sublime
Of grand resolves, projected feats,
When gaily decked the Ranger [11] meets
Proud ranks of hurlers that resort
To dare with him the manly sport.
He saw, in mind, his rivals yield
To Barrington [12] the well won field.

When, hark! upon the midnight clear
Rise booming sounds that strike his ear.

First indistinct and faintly booming,
Along the hills those sounds were coming;
Now scarcely heard in sullen languor,
   And wasted on the distant air,
   Returning echoes loudly bear
Upon the breeze their swelling clangor.
Briskly as the rain-drops pattering,
   When tropic clouds dissolve in showers,
   Rustling 'mid the leaves and flowers,
Thus was heard the rereward clattering,
Deep as the beat of rolling drum,
And murmuring as the queen-bee's hum.
Like aspen leaves rough breezes shaking,
The mountain sward around seemed quaking.
Along the matted tufts of broom
Young Connor's eye strained through the gloom;
His ear directs th' inquiring eye,
   Along the rugged mountain's breast,
Where the resplendent, moonlit sky
   Relieved its dark and serried crest.
Swift as the Borealis streak,
A horseman tops the highest peak,
A moment seen—and he was gone!
   Swift as those lurid lights divide
The ambient ether—hurrying on—
   The steed was reined by Connor's side.

" Hail, mortal! Ho, 'tis Connor's here !"
Commenced th' accosting cavalier,

" Fortune has smiled approving favours
And crowned the toil of long endeavours.
My Connor found—my mission's over—
List to the secrets I discover.
In Comber's Park, [18] this glorious night,
The fairies hurl by pale moonlight ;
A wager's laid, and for the bout
All things prepared, the ground marked out,
The goals arranged, yet, 'twould appear
My merrymen the issue fear.
Your prowess known in hurling sport,
Our fellow-hurlers of the Fort [14]
Resolved you should their contest share,
Urging that couriers should repair
   To seek you out wherever found.
They sought at home, abroad, where'er,
A Ranger could or might repair :
   Whilst in their search around,
They thought of merry Dysart's fair [15]
   And capered with you o'er that ground.
They drove your rivals from the green,
Guided the whirl of your *alpeen* ; [16]
In tents they sported through the dance,
   Tripp'd heel and toe, with rolling shuffle,
Crossed hands, in reels or jigs advance,
   And quick retire, by covering buckle. [17]
We nerved your free and lithesome limbs,
With frolic played off sportive whims,
We trust a nutshell slyly in
   The piper's broken-winded chanter,
Cracked the Cremona's treble string,

And raised the laughing dancer's banter.
We dived in overflowing methers,
We sailed through air on goss'mer feathers,
Purloined their heaps from apple-stalls
    And hopped them on each mortal's head,
Whilst, thick as hail, the volley falls
    Of brickbat loaves and gingerbread. [18]
Till, wearied with the long day's fun,
We hurried home at setting sun ;
But sought you first, and sought in vain
    Your form around the noisy green,
Hopeless of finding you, again
    The third time have I crossed this scene.
Then linger not—away to horse—
We'll sweep with speed our mountain course."

Nor more he said : but quickly braced
His fairy arm round Connor's waist,
And vaulting lightly on the steed,
Once more renewed his headlong speed.
Then wheeling round with vigorous bent,
The courser gained the rough ascent,
And snorting wildly sought his home,
With eye of fire and mouth of foam.
Whilst whip and rowel bring the tide
Of crimson down his tortured side,
Young Connor dreads the startling race,
Increased, if aught, at every pace.
In wild disorder past his eyes
Each object seen receding flies ;
The spiry grass, the heather flowers,

The mountain moss and *froghan* [19] berry
Spring from the courser's feet in showers,
  That rain along the path, where'er he
Plants the fast descending hoof
And hurls the broken soil aloof.
With every stretch of speed, the horse
  Like lightning leaps above the ground,
The mountain groans beneath the course,
  Sending an echo round and round.
The latent spark from flinty rock
The hoof relumes with every shock.
Air, earth and water, moon and sky,
In mingling parts, disruptured fly:
A thousand perils crowd that night,
Before the mortal's swimming sight.

The mountain top was gained and past,
  When sweeping down its eastern slope,
The Comber's Park was reached at last,
  Where wond'rous scenes successive ope
The visions of a fairy land:
  For thick as reeds upon the green,
  The moonlight shed a brilliant sheen
Above a vast, unnumbered band,.
That issued from the peopled Fort
To join in feats of hurling sport.
A silken vest of yellow hue,
A velvet cap, as azure blue,
  Bedecked one-half the train;
A scarlet cap and pea-green vest,
Relieved both jerkin loose and crest

Of even numbers that remain.
A common [20] from each shoulder hung,
A plume from every bonnet swung,
The plume, and hose, and doublet white,
Crowned every rich appareled wight.
Of dwarfish size and slender form
   These men of fairy land appear,
And endless seemed the crowds that swarm, [21]
   Clad in their bright and sportive gear.
Though mingled sounds and broken voices,
   Such as he heard at Dysart's fair,
   Struck on the mortal's listening ear,
Though dashed with fear, his soul rejoices,
   When " Welcome Connor, welcome here !"
   Burst in a loud, enlivening cheer.

Dismounting from the panting steed,
   The horsemen quick descend
And fairy bands the mortal lead,
   With his companion friend,
To hear the hurling roll called on
   By leaders of each band :
As fortune willed, in sportive bout,
   Together placed they stand.
His Island green young Connor graced,
His coarser frieze a garb displaced,
   With colours bright and gay :
Then quickly ranged, by bugle horn,
The leaders of each uniform
   Bring forth their men for play,
Disposed along the grassy field,

To win the palm or struggling yield.
The lists made out, the courses cleared,
For sporting feats the bands prepared,
Opposing staffs high banners reared,
   That showed the distant goal :
The ball was tossed aloft in air,
'Mid many a long, enlivening cheer,
And ardent hope or trembling fear
   Rose in each elfin soul.
The hurlets sweep above, around,
The groaning turf, with hollow sound,
   Rings 'neath their hurrying feet ;
And many a contest rises, where
The wiry shapes of elfins share
   The struggle, when their leaders meet.
The restless ball its course pursued
   By bat and stroke propelled,
And agonized with hope, they viewed
   The aerial path it held.
From north to south, from east to west,
It flew above the plain—nor rest
   When downward tending found :
The bands that wore the yellow vest,
Against the pea-green jackets prest,
   When to the rescue bound.
With jostling here and tripping there,
The shaking turf showed everywhere
   Its proof of prostrate forms ;
As toppling down, with headlong speed,
The inexperienced hurlers lead
   A sport that tires and warms.

An angry call—a shrilly cheer—
   As fortune turned the tide
Broke on the mortal's listening ear,
   From each opposing side;
The oft-repeated nervous stroke,
   From seasoned commons rung,
That proved them blades of ash or oak,
   By vigorous wielders swung.
Whilst over all, the pale moonlight
Gleamed on their glorious sports that night.

But 'midst their bands, o'ertopping all,
   The green of Connor's vest,
And swinging stroke, beneath the ball,
   Were marked by all the rest:
For like a meteor gleaming far,
He led the brunt of sportive war;
He swept like whirlwind o'er the course,
Though met by more than mortal force,
   His mortal might prevailed.
He crossed a limb, before each fay,
And sent him tottering far away,
   Till strength and muscle failed.
With shouldering shock, he urged along
Some eager sprite, that led the throng,
   To measure on the field,
His wiry shape of form and limb,
To rise in soiled, bespattered trim,
   Again to strive and yield.
But time and tide brought round reverse,
The chronicler must now rehearse,

How fall for fall was paid ;
The stroke, that bore the ball away,
Was stopped by many a tiny fay,
    The surge of victory stayed.
So culled the men—so brisk the game—
Not e'en a practised eye could gleam
Where victor's palm might seem t' incline
On wavering band or moment's time.

The hours ran by, and swiftly too,
The hurrying sportsmen eager flew
 Around the well-contested plain,
Their parts to play, their goal to gain,
    Till 'mid the glorious bout,
A nervous stroke propelled the flight
Of bandied ball across the sight,
    With hope-inspiring shout.
The horseman of the mountain course
Gave proof of his untiring force,
    As whizzed the ball in air ;
And as it stretched a lengthening arch,
Along its bow-bent, aerial march,
    There rose another cheer.
For Connor's bat resounds again,
Above the crowds of *gentlemen*, [22]
    That viewed this final stroke ;
A moment seen, and mounting high,
The ball was swept along the sky,
    Then through the bars it broke.

The game was won ! and deafening cheers
Salute the mortal's aching ears

From his victorious band;
When sullenly the conquered host
Retires amidst the taunting boast
  Of mortal beating fairy-land,
And bearing off the victor's wreath
  To deck a Ranger's brow.
Shame! shall their men himself beneath
  To Connor's boast allow?
But envy yields to nobler feeling,
When pleasure's tide, resistless stealing,
Tore from his foes their fierce defiance,
And merged all hearts in fond alliance.
For foe, as friend, his welcome pours
  On Connor's prowess tried,
And wildly joyous murmur roars
  Along the mountain's side;
Whilst hurrying to their hawthorn rath,
The fays direct their moonlit path,
To taste around the festive board
Those viands fairy realms afford.

The cloth was laid, was loaded, cleared,
  When vinous flaggons decked the board:
The sparkling glasses round appeared,
  And streams of nectar circling poured.
Whilst noisy revel rings among
The busy jovial guests that throng,
The mortal poured with open throat
His rhymeless verse and rustic note,
  And choirs repeat the strain,
With " Hip, hurrah!" and "nine times nine!"

A health was drunk from time to time,
 For Connor's hurling fame.
The festive riot swam at length
 Before his reeling eyes,
Till borne beyond his boozing strength
 Oblivious mists arise ;
And merry faces, known among
His boon companions, seem to throng
 By scores the crowded seats ;
When stealthily, as 'twere, he ends
By blending sprites with mortal friends,
 Whilst sober thought retreats.
Then looking round, by chance he spied
The fairy horseman at his side,
Who rising up, with eager haste,
And pointing to the bright'ning east,
The sprite of air immediate spoke
As Connor's consciousness awoke.

" Up, up, my friend, the day draws near,
The presages of morn appear,
 And pleasure's tide has run ;
Our steed awaits, with tireless force,
To try again your homeward course,
 With the declining moon.
Cast off your trappings and resume
 The frieze of silver grey ;
No longer can our bands presume
 Their revels to delay.
For we must close the fairy feast,
When the bright moon has sunk to rest ;

Whilst mortal eyelids close in sleep,
Alone their orgies fairies keep."

He said : when Connor soon obeyed
   And doffed his jerkin green,
Nor more his thoughts the time delayed
   By pondering on the scene ;
As chafed and champing forth was led
The charger, with impatient tread,
   That, doubly mounted then,
Flew off with all his former speed,
Whilst parting cheers pursue the steed,
   From crowds of *gentlemen.*
And far, the midnight breezes swell
An echoed " Connor, fare thee well !"

Now feast and feasters fade away,
Before the dawn of coming day ;
And, strange to say ! alone appears
The courser that his rider bears.
With thundering pace, the tireless horse
Swept o'er again the mountain course,
And leaping o'er ravines and rills,
An earthquake shakes the rugged hills.
Up crag and down, o'er plain and dell,
The charger's pattering hoof-plates fell,
   Till reined before an humble cot,
The mortal recognised his home,
And eagerly he hurried down
   To seek the well-known spot.
The spirit waved his last adieu

And off again like lightning flew.
The mortal raised the yielding latch
And strode beneath his roof of thatch;
Then sought the lowly pallet bed,
To rest his wearied, reeling head:
Nor more he knew, when languor deep
Spread o'er his eyes the seal of sleep.

But morning dawned, o'er hill and plain,
Leading the orb of day again,
    With warm and steady blaze
To mid-day's vertex, streaming on
The slothful subject of our song,
    Who dreamed of frisking fays.
He oped, at length, his heavy eyes,
And rising sought his garb of frieze,
But sought in vain the rustic dress,
    Nor frieze, nor silk, he found.
Yet quickly memory's clear impress
    Recalls the hurling ground,
Where festive sports of yestere'en
Ran riot 'neath the moonlight beam.
Half-clothed he returned where
The loss now felt he might repair:
And, lo! identified the prize
Of bundled homespun met his eyes.
Thus dressed, once more he seeks his home,
    Assured (as well he might
Infer) such tale must oft become
    The topic of a night,
When rustics round the peaty blaze

Should hear it told, in wild amaze,
And fear to venture homeward bound
Across the fairies' hurling ground.

Though many a past, revolving year
Dissolved the reign of elfin fear, [23]
Though hero and historian too
Have vanished long from mortal view,
Yet Cullenagh [24] remembers well
The tale old Connor loved to tell.
She guarantees the wond'rous truth
The sage related to her youth,
Who often yet rehearse the tale,
When daylight wanes along the vale ;
And who dare doubt, 'mongst sceptics, stood
The paragon of hardihood.

NOTES.

[1] So called, probably, from their marshy, fenny characteristics, as the Irish word, cuᴊᴊᴘⱸⱻ, *currach*, signifies a shrubby bog, marsh, or fen ; it is also applied to a race-course, a level plain, and a burial-ground.   The meaning of this word is explained in Cormac's Glossary. These meadows skirt the channel of the principal stream that flows westward from the Cullenagh mountains, by Kilvahan grave-yard.

[2] The beautiful demesne of Lewis Moore, Esq., who is said to be a lineal descendant of the former chieftains of Leix, forms a remarkable feature in the varied scenery, extending northward from the mountains of Cullenagh. Embosomed amidst the large trees in a particular portion of this finely-wooded demesne, are to be seen the ruins of an ancient church, the chancel of which contains the tombs of former representatives of this ancient family. In the reign of Queen Elizabeth, Cremorgan was held by Lishagh M'Mortogh Oge O'More and

his son Patrick, who joined Ony M'Rory O'More and his confederate rebels, at Stradbally; for which act Cremorgan became forfeited to the Queen and her successors, according to the Book of Leinster Inquisitions.

[3] The existing remains of Ballyknocken's quadrangular keep are at present in an extremely ruinous state. Only two sides of the old building have partially weathered the rough assaults of time and the still ruder attacks of hostile beleaguers. This castle, situated on the verge of a bog and in the middle of a plain surrounding it on all sides, appears to have had no peculiar defensive advantages of position. It was a dependency of the O'Moores, whose principal fortress was situated at Dunamase, over the great plain of Maryborough. During the progress of some excavations, which took place about thirty years ago, at a hill opposite the castle of Ballyknocken, several skeletons and portions of human remains were disinterred. Tradition had previously pointed out this place as the site of a former battle-field.

[4] This rocky eminence is a prominent object near the public road, leading from Stradbally to Abbeyleix, and it lies to the north-west of the Cullenagh mountains. It commands a fine view of the magnificently outlined Sliabh Bloom mountains, which separate the King's and Queen's counties. The rugged, yet verdant sides of Cashel Hill are covered with a luxuriant growth of copsewood and sweet pasturage.

[5] Cullenagh townland has doubtless given name to the barony in like manner denominated. This townland is situated in the parish of Ballyroan, Queen's county. Its three mountains are conspicuous objects for miles around, and they rise to a considerable elevation over the adjoining country. The townland is divided in two denominations, called respectively Cullenaghmore and Cullenaghbeg. The barony of Cullenagh forms one of the southern divisions of the Queen's county, and was formerly comprised within the ancient principality of Leix.

[6] A small townland lying to the north of the larger one of Cullenagh. Within the former an old grave-yard crowns the summit of a beautiful hill, and the burial ground is surrounded by a circular fosse and neglected fence, over which venerable hawthorns spread their verdant leaflets and fragrant blossoms in the summer season. The rich

pastures around are beautifully undulating, and afford abundant herbage for numerous flocks of sheep. A few upright marble-limestone tombs are kept in a highly polished state, from their constant contact with the unctuous fleeces of these animals that nestle and graze where—

> " The rude forefathers of the hamlet sleep."

Thomas O'Conor, one of the antiquarian staff, engaged on the Ordnance Survey of Ireland, supposed the original Irish name might be written, ᴄᵻᴸᴸ ᵯᵉᴀᴛᴏᵻᵻ, and become Anglicised as the *Church of St. Meathon.*

[7] The Black Mountain is the most elevated of the Cullenagh range. It is supposed to contain coal and other minerals, and several years ago mining operations were here commenced; but they have been long since discontinued. On the north side of this barren, peaty, heather-covered mountain, a large and solitary hawthorn tree hung over a small pond of water near the summit. It was called *Shed Bush,* and is remarkable on account of having been the appointed place for a gathering of the peasantry, about the commencement of the rising of 1798. A numerous band assembled there, partially armed with pikes and guns, but accomplished no greater amount of effective service, than did the king of France, who,

> " with twenty thousand men,
> Marched up the hill, and then came down again."

[8] The Middle Mountain, less elevated than the former, produces more abundant and nutritious pasturage, and is separated from the Black Mountain by a deep ravine, through which a rapid stream hurries in a succession of innumerable cascades. Some of these waterfalls are of considerable height, and uncommonly grand after heavy rains. A long, but narrow stripe of indigenous forest trees extends on either side of this ravine. About a century ago, these primeval woods were much more extensive, and were infested with wild cats and other destructive animals, as the older inhabitants of the country have heard from the accounts of their progenitors.

[9] The lowest and most fertile eminence of the three principal peaks. It is rather scrubby, but otherwise devoid of wood, and cultivated to some degree along the sides. Numerous flocks of sheep and

herds of cattle find an extended range along its base and more elevated ridges.

[10] The Foyle Pond is formed by the intercepted waters of that rivulet, which divides the Black and Middle Mountains. An exceedingly high and broad mound of earth and stone-work has been artificially constructed, to retain the storage water necessary for the mills, that are built at some distance below it; and from the steep and rugged banks rising above the Pond, the latter presents the appearance of a lone and narrow mountain lough, closed in on every side but the one, where the surplus waters escape over the solid abutment. Through this gorge of the ravine, a most varied and interesting vista of the lower plains, hills, and valleys of Kilvahan are seen to great advantage, from the head of Foyle Pond.

[11] A Cullenagh man even yet delights in this appellation, and the term is often applied to him by the inhabitants of surrounding districts. It arose from the circumstance of Sir Jonah Barrington's father having organized a cavalry corps, called the *Cullenagh Rangers*, during the memorable period of Irish volunteering. The full dress of these citizen soldiers was scarlet, and their undress white, with black velvet facings. This corps was for the most part enrolled from amongst the tenantry on the Barrington estates, and comprised a noble band of well mounted, athletic, and brave young men, officered by their patriarchal landlord and by his large family of sons, with a few gentlemen-farmers living on the property, who served as subalterns. Sir Jonah Barrington had been sent with a detachment of this body to attend the Grand National Convention of Ireland, which assembled in the Rotunda at Dublin, towards the close of 1783. At the head of those few men, Sir Jonah tells us, he felt prouder than an emperor, and that an impression was made on his youthful mind, which even in the chill of age was vivid and animating, whilst at the time, " a glowing patriotism, a military feeling, and an instinctive, though senseless lust for *actual service*, arose within him."—(*Rise and Fall of the Irish Nation*, chap. xviii.) Long before the writer of this Legend could have a knowledge of the historic incidents of the stirring period that called for an embodiment of these and similar brigades of volunteers, he often heard " in the days of childhood," the popular and truly

spirited strains of a favourite local song, which contained a threat that—

> "The French and the Spaniards, they might rue the day,
> When they'd face the bold Cullenagh Rangers."

It is rather strange, that Thomas MacNevin, in his *History of the Volunteers of* 1782, omits any description of the dress and equipments of the *Cullenagh Rangers*, one of the most effective and resolute corps ever enrolled, filled with an enthusiastic admiration and attachment towards their brave and popular colonel and officers, whilst ready to dare any enterprise under their command.

[12] The Barringtons appear to have been lords of the soil over Cullenagh and several other adjoining townlands, from the time of Queen Elizabeth to the close of the last century. According to the Leinster Inquisitions, John Barrington obtained letters patent, dated the 12th of May, in the sixth year of Queen Elizabeth's reign, conferring this manor on himself and his heirs male, in succession, after the original proprietors, the O'Moores of Leix, had been dispossessed. Towards the close of the last century, the Cullenagh property, incumbered by debts and mortgages, was sold to the late Sir John Parnell, Chancellor of the Irish Exchequer, and was afterwards transferred to the truculent and celebrated Judge Norbury, in whose family the proprietorship now remains. The Barringtons were exceedingly popular, and held an almost feudal sway over the affections and services of their numerous and comfortable tenantry. They were distinguished by a fondness for horsemanship and field-sports, especially for the favourite game of hurling. They obtained still greater notoriety for their duelling propensities, and were generally known by the appellation of the *Fighting Barringtons*. It is said, that Lady Barrington, the mother of Sir Jonah and his numerous band of brothers, was accustomed to practise candle-snuffing with duelling-pistols herself, and to teach her sons the most effective methods of dealing out death or wounds to adversaries that might dare to offer or accept cartels. Her theories and practice were afterwards fully illustrated, by the death of more than one of her sons in the *duello :* and nearly all of them had frequent experience of single combat, either as seconds or principals. The only scion of intellectual eminence belonging to this family was

the celebrated Sir Jonah Barrington, Judge of the Admiralty, an eloquent speaker in the Irish Parliament, and the author of several popular works. The facetious baronet's *Personal Sketches* of his own time, are exceedingly amusing, and contain many interesting family anecdotes, characteristic of the social state of Ireland over sixty years ago, although several humorous etchings are over-coloured and to say the least greatly exaggerated. The old baronial-looking residence of the Barringtons is now uninhabited, and the winds whistle through its desolate, unroofed walls, and over its antique gables. Some thirty years back, an exiled member of this family, living in France, had expectations of establishing his claims to the proprietorship of the paternal estates, and sent a characteristic circular to the tenantry living thereon, to pay no rent to the *de facto* landlord, assuring them that " the crack of a Barrington's whip would be heard once more on the Cullenagh mountains." The announcement created the greatest enthusiasm amongst tenants on the Cullenagh property; but the promise has never been fulfilled, nor is there a fair prospect of its being realized at any future period.

[13] A beautiful green paddock on the eastern slope of the Black Mountain, formerly a favourite hurling field with the men of Cullenagh, who under the training of the Barringtons attained a renowned degree of proficiency at this invigorating, but rather dangerous exercise. Parishes, baronies, and counties often contended for victorious laurels, at this truly national sport, and vast crowds of the brave and fair assembled as spectators on these occasions. The men of Cullenagh were rarely matched, and still more rarely excelled, by their opponents. Their numerous contests were celebrated by the local ballad-mongers in songs that are yet popular, although not often perfect in metrical structure or poetic merit. Even the hurling gentry of the day were more celebrated for their prowess at field sports, than by their literary or intellectual capabilities. One of the most notorious, amongst the sporting gentlemen of the Queen's county, having obligingly complied with the request of a brother sportsman, who desired to complete a certain number of efficient hurlers for an important match then pending, sent a contingent of half-a-dozen athletes, with an accompanying note, containing these words, " Enclosed I send you six of the best

hurlers in all Ireland." It proved rather fortunate—yet still inexplicable—that the note was delivered by hand; for even in these days of cheap postage, the size and weight of such an epistle, directed through the post-office, would press rather heavily on the finances, either of the sender or receiver.

[14] A name given by the peasantry to one of the many raths, so generally scattered over the surface of our island. These forts or raths are supposed to be the favourite residences of the fairies.

[15] The two annual fairs of Dysart are held on Whit-Monday and on the 12th of November. In times past, those fairs were disturbed by faction and party fights, which often ended with bloodshed and homicide. The fair-green was situated on one of these elevated ridges in the Dysart range of hills, near the graveyard and the now deserted Protestant Church of the parish of Dysart Enos. A noted local celebrity, some years since deceased, and a retired octogenarian captain of Dragoons, who had formerly witnessed some active service in the British army, felt an instinctive passion to behold a good, heady fight, on the periodical recurrence of Dysart fair, and he regularly attended as a veteran volunteer, to lend assistance in marshalling the array and directing the evolutions of contending factions. He generally sided with the weaker party, and when his men were obliged to give way before an assault of their opponents, the Captain would usually cry out, at the top of his voice: " Boys, don't desert your colours, but rally round the Church!" He always felt very indignant, when the police attended in sufficient force to prevent an engagement or to overawe the combatants, and asseverated on the honour of a soldier, that the bravery and spirit of the peasantry would evaporate, if these guardians of the public peace could succeed in arresting the single-stick play of blackthorn and shillelagh. He disapproved of stone-throwing during the progress of the fight; but when a volley of missiles flew around him, whilst mounted on a splendid hunter he directed the onset, a quick eye and a graceful, agile turn of the body usually protected him from an aimless stroke, never intended for his injury—the good-natured officiousness he displayed on these occasions having been always duly appreciated by the belligerents. The business transactions of Dysart fair commonly ended at noon, the remainder of

the day being devoted to amusement or rioting, in "the good old times." The heroic days of this once celebrated green have departed, and are long since numbered amongst things that were: the lowing of cattle, the squeaking of sucking pigs, and the bleating of sheep resound over the fertile and verdant hills of this romantic vicinage, instead of the *shibboleth* of party and the wild *abu* of contending factions. The finely-wooded demesne and elegant mansion of Lamberton Park, the seat of Michael Sweetman, Esq., lie between the Dysart hills and the Cullenagh mountains. Lamberton was formerly a possession of a celebrated jurist and anti-union orator in the Irish Parliament, the Right Honorable Arthur Moore, late Judge of the Common Pleas. Sir Walter Scott, during his visit to Ireland, spent some time as the guest of Judge Moore at Lamberton Park, and felt greatly delighted with the scenic beauties of this neighbourhood.

[16] A stout and well-seasoned stick used by the peasantry in faction fights.

[17] These are feats of agility and movements commonly exhibited in the dances of our countrymen.

[18] The faries are said to delight in frolics of this nature on Irish fair greens, but their forms are invisible to human eye, during the perpetration of these practical jokes.

[19] The Irish name given to the *vaccinium myrtillus*, bilberrry, which grows profusely on the sides and summit of the most elevated mountain of the Cullenagh range. This berry forms a part of the autumnal food of grouse, and is often used in making tarts. Its collection by the young people affords an inducement or an excuse for many pleasant excursions to the highlands, when it has fully ripened with the advancing season.

[20] The name given to the wooden instrument, used by the most expert hurlers. It was generally made of seasoned ash, thus combining the qualities of endurance and lightness. The handle was smoothly fashioned and round; the extremity of the *common* was crooked, and flattened on both sides.

[21] The faries are generally represented as gregarious in their pastimes and movements. Their favourite costume is a high-peaked or conical cap, and sometimes a three-cornered or shovelled one,

with a plume of feathers depending: they wear a scarlet and gold-laced uniform and long boots, in military fashion, and are mounted on steeds whilst travelling. The jingling of steel curbs and the clattering of dangling sword-scabbards are sure to attract the attention of a belated wight in some lone dingle. Sometimes gorgeous helmets and glittering drawn swords are seen as the cavalcade gallops silently along, or engages in the customary equestrian evolutions of military tactics. Such apparitions are usually witnessed in the immediate neighbourhood of their raths, which often open to give the horsemen exit or entrance. Although seen on certain occasions in the gloaming of evening, their military excursions most frequently take place under the veil of night, and the full moonlight best reveals their gambols to the eye of mortals. Astride on branches of trees or skipping from bough to bough, they also appear to the bewildered gaze of affrighted travellers. They have favourite tracks or gaps through which they invariably pass on their route. It likewise happens, that indiscriminate crowds of fairies, male and female, sweep by those stations with the rapidity of lightning; when those who have been abducted from earth can be seen, and if grasped by a friend, placed in a suitable position, may be restored once more to their families. Great dexterity and strength are required on the part of the person attempting a rescue, which, if unsuccessful, subjects his fairy friend to the harsh treatment of elfin companions and to additional surveillance, lest a renewal of such effort should again be made. The fairy doctors, men and women, pretend that by their incantations they can tell the exact time when a lost friend will pass with the fairy host, through one of these well known passages, and that they can enable a living friend to witness the procession, so as by ingenuity and courage he may embrace such opportunity to effect a seizure.

[22] To deprecate the anger or mischievous propensities of fairies, the peasantry are accustomed to call them *gentlemen, good people,* &c. These titles are supposed to flatter their vanity, in case the invisible elves should be within hearing. The Scottish Highlanders entertain a like superstition.

[23] Although these lines in the present legend had been composed, long before the writer was gratified by a perusal of Denis

Florence Mac Carthy's inimitably beautiful fairy tale, entitled *Alice and Una*, there is a cognate idea, but far more felicitously expressed, in the following opening stanza of our gifted countryman's highly poetical romance of Ceim-an-eich :

> " Ah, the pleasant time hath vanished, ere our wretched doubtings banished
> All the graceful spirit-people, children of the earth and sea,
> Whom in days now dim and olden, when the world was fresh and golden,
> Every mortal could behold in haunted rath, and tower, and tree—
> They have vanished, they are banished—ah ! how sad the loss for thee,
>   Lonely Ceim-an-eich !"

[24] Tradition has preserved a popular opinion, that the etymon Cullenagh was so given, because of the large holly which formerly grew in its extensive woods : this statement was communicated by an old and intelligent farmer, Laurence Byrne of Fallybeg, a friend of the late Dr. O'Donovan. A castle formerly stood on the lands of Cullenagh, according to local statements ; and on the revised Ordnance Survey Maps of Ireland, the site of an abbey is indicated on the upper acclivities of the Black Mountain.

No. VI

A Legend of Donegal.

—

THE INVISIBLE SEA-CASTLE.

WITH ev'ning shades descending,
A hooker's sail was bending
The mast to those white cots that stood by clear fountains,
Whilst ocean's mists were blending
Their vaporous hues o'er the Donegal mountains.

The sunset shadows hover
The rereward ocean over,
Whilst on shore might be seen the fisherman's daughter,
Scanning the sail-spread rover,
Careering along the horizon of water.

Those hardy sailors, crowding
On spars their canvas shrouding,
Were sons of the soil in their lov'd Inishowen,
Constant as skies overclouding
They clung to their hills like the wild native rowan.

Lo ! 'twixt the bark and highland,
Their own enchanted island,
Its green shore extends to the kisses of ocean,
Becalmed mid the sky and
The light azure wave with its tremulous motion.

Above the verdant bowers
Arise embrasured towers, [1]
Relieved by dark shades of the far mountain broom ;
   Whilst fragrant shrubs and flowers
Shed o'er the wild waves their fresh evening perfume.

'Twas the islet castle haunted
By spirit forms enchanted,
That roamed after death through bowers of bent willow ;—
   Its view never granted
To a race, save the one, that now sailed on the billow.

In the walls are deep'ning reaches,
Where symmetrically niches
Awne over some marble wrought figures—when Hesper
   Sheds his last glow—while the screeches
Of cormorants herald their homeward-bound vesper.

The chill and oozing dew-damp
Of an overspreading yew stamp
On those statues a shade of cold charnel impress ;
   With lurid light, a blue lamp
Of dark lazuli swings from each green leafy tress.

And thus by waning skylight
Of a duskly-gleaming twilight,
The O'Dougherty spectres of chieftain and vassal
   Loom on the sailors' eye-sight,
Who are clansmen of wardens spell-bound in that castle.

A day shall yet dissever
From thrall those shapes for ever,
And from bondage that clouded their primitive glory:
When waked again, they never
Must die till their deeds be recorded in story. [2]

But night has come! and ocean's
Phosphoric commotions
Beat round the seamen, whilst the rising blast seizes
Those hallucinating notions
That depart with a sweep of the fresh'ning breezes.

And the swelling billow washes
Their prow with bursting plashes,
As the fisher nears shore, with his Gaelic orison;
Till in sheltered cove he lashes
The hooker, that sped o'er the watery horizon. [3]

NOTES.

[1] The enchanted castle of the O'Doughertys has a fabled existence off the coast of Donegal, and far out on the Atlantic Ocean. It
is invisible to all, except those bearing the name of the former chiefs
and clansmen of Inishowen. The description of its appearance on
the Ocean Island corresponds with that attempted in this legend.
Tradition holds, that marble statues to be seen with girded swords
and ranged within the walls are veritable effigies of chieftains and
warriors belonging to the renowned race of the O'Doughertys, who,
by some strange enchantment, were metamorphosed into stone, at a
period long remote. When those spells shall be broken, the inanimate
statues are to resume their former vigour and condition, to draw their
swords, and recover possession of a lost inheritance. This legend is

somewhat similar to one which Charles Gavan Duffy relates in his introduction to the fine ballad of Iɴɪʀ Cóʒaɪɴ, viz., that a troop of Hugh O'Neill's horse lies enchanted and in a lethargic trance, within a cave, under the hill of Aileach. The horsemen only wait to have this spell removed, in order to wave their swords once more for the liberation of Ireland.

[2] The Scottish borderers have a tradition, that Thomas of Her-sildoune, surnamed the Rhymer, remains enchanted in the land of Faery; but, that he will return to earth, during some future great convulsion of society, and then accomplish various distinguished achievements, is also believed. In Dr. John Leyden's *Scenes of Infancy*, Part i., we find the following allusions to this superstition, bearing a striking affinity to the incidents recorded in our present legend :

> "Mysterious Rhymer, doomed by fate's decree,
> Still to revisit Eildon's fated tree :
> When oft the swain, at dawn of Hallow-day,
> Hears thy fleet barb with wild impatience neigh ;
> Say who is he, with summons long and high,
> Shall bid the charmed sleep of ages fly,
> Roll the long sound through Eildon's caverns vast,
> While each dark warrior kindles at the blast."

[3] Some sailors of the O'Dougherty family, being overtaken by a violent tempest, when far out on the Atlantic, endeavoured, but in vain, to reach the mainland of Donegal. The storm increased and the waves rose in mountains; their frail bark was speedily overwhelmed in the waters of the ocean. At the moment when these mariners gave themselves up for lost, their enchanted island appeared to emerge from out its waters, and they were cast on shore, by the violence of this tempest. The first object, which appeared to their view, was the enchanted castle with its spell-bound tenants. The sailors attempted to draw a sword from the sheath of the most conspicuous image, when this figure motioned them away, saying, at the same time, the day had not yet arrived when that sword was to be drawn. By a strange tissue of circumstances, the adventurers were enabled to gain their homes on the coast of Donegal, where they afterwards related this wild and romantic story.

No. VII.

A Legend of Bishop's Island, River Barrow.

THE TREASURE DREAM.

THRICE in a stranger's dream came the fond vision:
  Then with hope as his guide, he set out on the morrow,
For a green lonely Isle [1] of an aspect Elysian,
  With its treasures that lay, in the bosom of Barrow.

Nor long ere he found the fair scene of his dreaming,
  When toil-worn and spent had the traveller wandered,
For he reached that lone Island, an evening sun streaming
  Bright rays on the gold flood that round it meandered.

And the soul and the sense were enraptured with pleasure,
  Whilst his golden ideal had haunted the rover,
Re-assuring the grasp of a limitless treasure,
  All his fond wishes crowned and his wayfaring over.

Envious fame blew the trumpet of threatening and danger,
  He recked not of hearing when living afar;
And it seemed as if fortune had drawn for that stranger
  His lot 'neath the gleam of some pestilent star.

Rude churls of Barrow had vowed that its treasure,
  For their own favoured race near its waters should lie, and
Defensively stood, till his parting steps measure
  The dreamer's retreat from their treasure-trove Is-
    land. [2]

NOTES.

[1] Bishop's Island is included, with the townland of Derry-oughter West, of which it forms part, in the parish of Ballybrackan, on the county Kildare side of the river Barrow. It is situated about midway between Cloney Castle, near the bridge of Dunrally, and Riverstown House and Demesne. Within the latter enclosure, St. Bridget's well is pointed out, and a *pattern* or patron, formerly held there, was attended by the peasantry from even distant parts of the country. Bishop's Island is separated from the mainland by a very narrow and probably an artificial channel. Several ridges appear about the centre of this long and low-lying island, the surface of which is covered with rank grass and small shrubs. Long bulrushes wave over the water around its sides. In former times, it was possibly a defensive position, as we find, even at present, a rath situated very near it, on the Kildare side of the silvery Barrow.

[2] The foregoing legend I have heard related by a peasant boy, who pointed out to me the presumed spot on this Island, where the pilgrim dreamer intended to commence his excavations. I was likewise informed, that several attempts had been made by the Kildare people to unearth the occult treasure, but hitherto without any success. During the raids and civil broils, which so frequently disturbed the social state of this country, there is every reason to believe that valuables were oftentimes secreted or buried in the ground for greater security. Numerous accidents might have happened to remove the slightest clue to any chance of obtaining these real or imaginary treasures. There can be no doubt, that many an Irish father has given *bona fide* mandate to his sons, similar in substance to that conveyed in the words of La Fontaine:

> " Un trésor est caché dedans.
> Je ne sais pas l'endroit ; mais un peu de courage
> Vous le fera trouver : vous en viendrez à bout.
> Remuez votre champ dès qu'on aura fait l'août :
> Creusez, fouillez, bêchez, ne laissez nulle place
> Où la main ne passe et repasse."

Fables Choisies. Liv. v. Fab. ix.

No. VIII.

A Legend of Blarney.

THE LEPRECHAWN.

How pleasing at the close of day
Down through those vales to stray
  Where Blarney's towers
    Frown o'er the wildering woods,
      And cast their shadow on the floods. [1]
  When leaves and flowers
  Adorn bright bowers
In the full prime of summer bloom,
Whilst faintly through the welkin peers the rising moon,
And nature's calm repose hath shrouded hill and glade
With mellowed tints of colour deepening on to darker shade.

    'Tis a weird scene!
To view the ancient keep rise proud and grand,
Even in its ruined state, above a smiling land,
    Where lawns of green
    Spread out between
  The leafy-belted Martin's rushing course,
And the wild mountain-cradled Shournagh, murmuring
hoarse,
  Leaping like eager steeds in full career,
  To join their parted currents, strong yet clear.
    Reflecting copse and brake,
    Still was the waveless lake;

And oak-trees rising tall
As the embattled wall,
With giant knotted branches, spreading firm and large,
Round the smooth surface of its grassy marge.

Florence Mac Carthy was the peasant hight,
Who wandered forth by evening's misty light,
Treading the tangled mazes of the wood,
In pensive, solitary, sentimental mood,
For Muire, fair and pure, he loved and wooed ;
And as he rambled there
Built castles in the air
Higher by far than Blarney's lordly turrets stood.

Still as he wandered on
Noonlight into dusk had gone.
All the more potent proved the spell
That led his thoughts to coming time.
Who but a lover could the motive tell
Which to a mellowed strain known words combine,
Witching as the patriot lady's lay [2]
In light and dulcet measure,
Cheering with note subdued the lonely way
His soul enraptured with some dreamy pleasure.
And as he trod
Along the verdant sod,
The woods around
In cadence sweet resound
Those tripping couplets, arch,
That softly sweet so lightly march

In metre to the *aria* of *Kate Kearney*;
    Hark! from the thickets near,
    Though no minstrel did appear,
Another tune more plaintive struck the ear,
For the song that echo gave described the *Groves of Blar-
ney.* [8]
        And its well remembered strain,
        To the scene was quite germane.

        "Tick-tack, tick-tack," [4]
        With sharp and rapid crack,
Is also heard, but fainter through the groves,
        When stealing on tip-toe
        With bated breath and slow
Florence neared a hazel thicket's green alcoves.
        Then seated in the shade [5]
        In quaintest fashion placed
        On his low stool, arrayed
        With beaver cocked and laced [6]
A curly powdered wig emerging from its leaf,
Appeared a grotesque figure and a wrinkled face,
Thickly as bearded barley bristles in the harvest sheaf,
Set o'er in furrows deep, with every strange grimmace.
        As damsons black and ripe enow
        Fall from their stems, the urchin's prize,
        A low and heavy beetled brow
        Hung darkly o'er his leering eyes.
        Full o'er his parted mouth, down-hooked,
        A monstrous nose and rubicund,
        Like the old eagle's beak, grew crooked
        On to the pointed chin, it scarcely shunned.

Nor like the close and regular row
Which young and modish galliards show,
Nor with the orient pearl's lustre shine,
His teeth, all isolated, ranged in jagged line.

Dun was the garb he wore,
And buttoned loose before
Over a showy vest,
Full frilled above his breast.
Light as the zephyr wind,
Long trailed his skirts behind.
Sprucely as any antiquated *beau,*
He wore a stock and collar falling low.
His velveteens encased
The lower limbs, so tightly braced;
Of snow-white hue, the silken hose,
Drawn o'er his tapering legs, relieve the laquer-polished
shoes,
Strapped down with clasps of gold,
Most gorgeous to behold.

And near were seen those instruments of trade,
For the cordwainer's use especial made,
Pegs, pincers, tacks, sharp knives and awls,
Heel-tippings, lasts, and waxen balls,
Whilst various shapes of leather strewed the ground,
And tiny shoes [7] were scattered loose around.
But whilst the craftsman sung
His elbows wide were swung,
And firm the waxen lines he strung.

The awl was often plied,
In the sewing process tried ;
And closing many a seam,
Rapid as if he wrought with more complex machine.
Anon, the wight his hammer took,
It works with light, repeated tap,
While beneath the lapstone shook
And sounded on the hero's lap ;
But quite unconscious still, a mortal stood so near,
To gaze upon his busy toil, his chant to overhear,
With epiglottis straining much, wild notes he forced to
pass so
Like a *maestro's* highest quaver, sinking down to deepest
basso.

Whilst with stealthy pace and sudden spring,
His elbows braced and arms slowly swing,
Florence momently resolved his plan,
And he pounced upon the tiny man
For he knew it was the Leprechawn
That had sought a cozy corner, near the spreading lawn.
Florence meant to hold him fast, until bright gold,
In quantity untold,
Should replenish, from the *fairy's purse*, [8]
A *sporan*, [9] lightly stocked, which from slender grew to
worse.

Held choking by the neck
The dwarf was quickly jerked on high,
Against the ruddy clouds that fleck
With blinding rays the western sky.
And the mortal bent a stern eye

On the wight's contorted face,
Not much improved with every wild grimmace,
Which told of mingled terror and malignant hate,
Whilst vainly struggling to escape this crisis of his fate.

" Come, Mr. Leprechawn,
No hand shall be withdrawn,"
Cried Florence, "till you show that purse of gold,
Of which you take such care,
And liberally share
The treasure that so jealously you hold ;
I don't mean to be hard,
If you decently reward
A friend for kind attentions to such a wealthy creature.
Should you hope to get away,
Your earnest wish I'll not gainsay,
As I'm sure a captive's life would prove trying to your
nature ;
I'll give my truthful vow,
I should not ask you even now
To part with what both man and sprite hold dear ;
Need I then those lines rehearse
That tell of money getting scarce,
And threatening future hardship, when Leprechawns ap-
pear. [10]
My rent now due, I count on you, for means to pay this
gale,
And settle her, I love full well, in comfort on my farm,
'Twere mercy sure, to aid the poor, when friends and mo-
ney fail—
To cure past ills and cancel bills, that prelude future harm."

" Well then, Florence Mac Carthy,"
Cried the dwarf, " as blithe and hearty,
You've found a treasure on this blessed eve,
Take what you've fairly won, and then I'll take my leave ;
For the future cease to grieve.
If you wish to meet the rent,
With something as a dower on a wife well spent,
This purse will more than pay for all, and I am quite con-
 tent."
Then, from his pocket vest
A weighty, swelling purse he took,
And thrust it forth in haste
To meet his captor's eager look.
" Ho !" cried Florence, " open wide the upper band,
And let me see the sum thus placed at my command."
" Friend," said the Leprechawn, " trust my word."
" No, I never," Florence cried, " do anything absurd."
Remonstrance proving vain,
A glance of proud disdain,
With gathering anger on the mortal's curving brow,
Obliged the wily sprite to undo the opening now.
What doth Florence there behold ?
No coins of sterling gold,
But copper tokens large and of value much debased.
Instant, in rage he threw
That purse away from view,
Which sunk beneath the Shournagh's placid surface there
 displaced.

Fury beaming in his eyes,
And wrathful speech upon his tongue,

Once more the wriggling prize,
By Florence held aloof and high in air was hung. [11]
" Then," spoke the dwarfish elf,
" To no living mortal but yourself
Would I trust this secret of the fairies' horde
Which all earthly comforts can afford,
Destined luxuries for one
Who will delve beneath yon cone
Where waves the single yellow-blossomed *bohilawn:*
If you wish a fortune made,
Hasten quickly for your spade,
Your luck improve, friend Florence," cried the wily Lepre-
chawn. [12]

" No, your words I value not,
Nor shall I mark that spot,
For often have I heard, should you vanish from man's sight ;
Whole roods of yellow weed
Would blossom forth with speed,
Nor could he find that place, where rests your gold so
bright."

" Nay then," rejoined the sprite,
" I question not a right
To fix your gaze upon me though firmly spell-bound ;
Yet loose this hold, I pray
Whilst we walk along the way,
Till we find your spade to open wide those treasures under
ground.
Then, fear not my escape, when I move your steps before,
Soon shall we both return again to lift that golden store."

Florence, keeping well his eyes upon the Leprechawn,
Laid him lightly on the green and grassy lawn,
When forth the little sprite moved first with measured pace
Through devious paths and hanging woods,
Over plains, around the lake, back to the Shournagh's floods
He drew the mortal after him in this fatiguing chase: [13]
As glowing rays of setting sunlight fell
From the broad shield of fire,
And blaze ere they expire
On Blarney's topmost towers, over every mossy dell,
With gleaming splendour o'er the streams,
In lengthening trace, the rippling surface beams.
Up and down the grassy knowes
By the caves and sweet *Rock Close* [14]
The dapper son of Crispin moved and Florence followed fast,
Nor winced a glance one moment, lest that view should
be his last.

Still on the panting mortal came
Like a beagle after game,
Where proudly o'er its basement rock
Oft hath the castle-bastions stood the battle shock,
When from their loop-holes rang the arquebuss,
And sped the deadly bullet on a foe,
Few raiders ventured o'er Muskerry's fosse,
Such missiles dealing death on those below.
Now are its crennelled tops quite tempest worn
Shattered its thickest walls by cannon torn.
Though lonely as it stands and sadly desolate,
Time spares his land-marks yet, from their long threaten-
ing fate. [15]

Deep ditch and thick-set hedge,
High wall and craggy ledge,
Lightly the gnome bounded over:
But like the fox unearthed from his cover
Before the baying hound
And the clanging bugle sound,
So Florence vaulted every mound
And fence and knoll of ground,
Still keeping full in view each movement of the rover,
But vainly called, while threatening much to wreak his
vengeance dire,
On the old-fashioned squire,
Should he not halt such tireless speed and wild career:
For aimless seemed the course
Through thorns and jagged gorse
Which tracked with blood of Florence those paths through
which they steer.

At length, within an overhanging wood,
The Leprechawn, one moment faltering stood,
And peering backwards through the distant shade,
Cried, " Yonder glides an arch and a merry maid,
Muire O'Driscoll fair
Lingers for some lover there."

It was the trysting hour and favourite spot,
Nor were the plighted vows of Florence soon forgot.
He sudden glanced behind
But Muire's form he sought in vain:
Then on the evening wind
Loud screams of mocking laughter ring again:

Aghast he turned to gaze, when sobered thought could
dawn
　　On his sore burthened mind:
　　Nor trace can Florence find
Which might denote the course of his vanished Lepre-
chawn.

NOTES.

[1] The celebrated castle and demesne of Blarney are situated
near a village bearing the like name, within a few miles of the city of
Cork. The rivers Martin and Shournagh, as likewise some other
streams descending from the Bogra mountains, join their waters to
the Blarney river, before its final confluence with the river Lee.
Eastwards the Comane bog extends, and during the earlier part of
the last century it was a trackless wilderness. From the upper bat-
tlements of Blarney Castle, a very fine prospect of the adjoining
grounds and their natural features may be obtained. There is a
small lake in the centre of this demesne.

[2] Allusion is here made to a beautiful lyric of Sydney Lady
Morgan, to whom all true Irishmen owe a deep debt of gratitude, for
her literary abilities, advocacy and devoted exertions on behalf of this
Island and its much misrepresented and calumniated inhabitants.

[3] The humourously burlesque and graphic poetical effusion,
which commences with these lines,

> "The groves of Blarney they are so charming,
> All by the purling of sweet silent streams,"

is usually attributed to a citizen of Cork, Richard Alfred Milliken, who
wrote it about the year 1798 or 1799. The air and words of this
popular song soon attained a very extended range of celebrity. The
lines, however, underwent various mutations; and they must long
continue to excite the risible faculties of the erudite classicist, as of
the unlettered humourist, in a " polyglot edition" set forth in *The*

Reliques of Father Prout. Besides the vernacular, we there find translations into Greek, Latin, French and Italian, in which the spirit and character of the original are wonderfully rendered. Another rhapsody, of a nearly similar import, runs in these opening lines:

> " O Blarney Castle, my darling,
>   Sure you're nothing at all but a stone, &c."

Further particulars, regarding the composition of these famous ditties, may be found in Crofton Croker's *Popular Songs of Ireland.*

[4] " Tick-tack, tack-tack," is a sound usually heard from the beating of a Leprechawn's lapstone, before the sprite himself comes into view.

[5] The Leprechawn of Leinster is a spirit of pigmy size and lonely habits. He is supposed to be the fairies' shoemaker, and when busily engaged at his handicraft, he is often surprised by mortals. He has a knowledge of where all hidden and earth-buried treasures lie concealed. He is generally found in the evening's gloaming, and sometimes by moonlight, seated on a tiny shoemaker's stool with all its furnishings, behind a thickly-planted hedge-row or within an unfrequented wood, usually in a retired situation. The fear of capture by mortals always haunts him. But as he is ingenious in framing devices to effect his escape, few succeed in procuring the buried treasures, which they would wish him to reveal, whilst placed under compulsion and threats of death. It is necessary to keep the eye fixed on him, until the treasure appears to view. He will pretend that some danger or an enemy threatens the captor from behind, or that some extraordinary appearance presents itself, to induce the mortal to look in another direction. If he once succeed in effecting such result, the Leprechawn immediately vanishes. To this tradition our national bard alludes in one of his *Irish Melodies:*

> "Like him the sprite,
>   Whom maids by night
> Oft meet in glen that's haunted.
> Like him, too, beauty won me,
> But while her eyes were on me,
>   If once their ray
>   Was turned away,
> Oh! winds could not outrun me."

[6] The Leprechawn wears a low-crowned, broad-leafed and three-cornered cocked hat, with silver band. The *Louis Quatorze* style of court dress gives a tolerable idea of his frilled shirt, long embroidered vest, trimmed body coat, velveteen silver-buckled breeches, silk stockings and square-toed cordevan shoes, strapped over with gold braces and buckles. A red night-cap forms a part of the Leprechawn's working dress at times; and drab or grey is a favourite colour for his principal habiliments. Like other members of his fraternity, he often enlivens the taps on his lapstone or the pulling of his waxed ends, with a merry lilting melody or catch. Sometimes the Leprechawn, in his hurry to escape or through forgetfulness, leaves the shoes he is making behind him, when they are found by the peasantry and preserved as objects of curiosity. Smoking and drinking are his special propensities. He is said to be avaricious, reserved, cunning and cowardly. In the province of Munster, this dwarfish sprite is variously called the Luricaune, Cluricaune or Lurigadaune, and in Ulster, he is known as the Loghery Man.

[7] Sometimes the Leprechawn will obligingly heel or sole boots and shoes, belonging to mortals, if they are left near his haunts.

[8] This supernatural son of Crispin is thought to possess a little leather purse, which is always carried about his person. It contains a shilling, called Sprè na Skillenagh, or the Shilling Fortune. Sprè, literally means *cattle*, and by metonymy, *money;* as the old Irish paid a marriage dower or gift, not in coin, but in cattle, the chief source of wealth amongst a pastoral people. No matter how often this coin may be expended, it is always found replaced in the purse, thus according with the nursery story, which tells us that

> " Fortunatus of Cyprus
> Met dame Fortune in plenty,
> She gave him a purse
> That would never be empty."

The Leprechawn, however, carries another purse, filled with worthless brass coins. The apparent weight at first fills the receiver with pleasurable anticipations, but when this purse is examined, the cunning sprite has already disappeared, and the prize is comparatively worthless.

[9] This Irish name, Sponán, signifies *a purse.*

[10] When a Leprechawn is seen by any person, a hard summer or evil times may be anticipated. Hence the distich so well known to the peasantry :

> " When Leprechawns appear,
> Troubled times are near."

[11] The true way for grasping a Leprechawn is to seize.him by the nape of the neck, and then hold him fixed between one's eyes and the sun. If the eyes be kept direct upon him, and if money be perseveringly demanded, it will be granted : yet such consummation is a matter of no easy accomplishment.

[12] When all hope fails of inducing his tormentor to avert the eyes, the Leprechawn points out a spot near some particular thorn, bush, weed, or other remarkable object in a field, which is notched or marked in such a manner, that it may be readily identified, according to the adventurers' supposition. The Leprechawn is then thoughtlessly released by the credulous mortal, whose next object must be to seek a spade, in order to dig out the looked for treasure. On returning, the whole space around that spot is covered with such a multiplied quantity of *fac similes* to the object originally marked, that no distinguishing characteristic can be traced, so that further search would prove useless, and all hopes of acquiring a fortune must be abandoned.

[13] He thus leads from one field to another as a ruse to direct attention from him, and he generally endeavours to escape by climbing ditches or by causing delay.

[14] In a small and romantic dell, called the Rock Close, the visitor is strangely gratified with a combination of neglected artificial and natural local features, terminated by a rocky terrace, rising over the river, which calmly glides beneath the feet. The rocks are trelissed over with moss, creeping ivy and wild brambles. An irregular flight of rude, stone steps, known as the " Witch's Stairs," descends through the solid rock ; and the explorer will find his future passage barred on the river banks, over which some trees spread their graceful and pendant branches. The castle itself rises nobly on an isolated lime-stone rock, at the junction of two rivers ; and near its top the celebrated " Blarney Stone" is pointed out, on its north-eastern angle. The curious properties of this stone, if unknown to strangers,

are sure to be related by the attendant guide. The grounds are still very beautiful although sadly neglected. Oak, beech, ash, birch, and alder are found in great variety. Most of the former walks and passages are choked with thorns, but in the summer season they are spread over with wild flowers and almost every species of botanic plants. Beneath the castle there are certain natural caverns. Some of the early castellans had one of these converted into a dungeon, in which several massive iron rings and bolts have remained. This cave is entered by a very strong door, and only a single window admitted a dim light to the wretched captives. Within these caverns, very interesting and beautifully formed stalagmites and stalactites are grouped in fantastic shapes. A picturesque bridge, which led to the castle, has been swept away by the wintry and mountain torrents, and the statues " gracing this noble place in," have been removed, for many past years. To crown this picture of desolation, much of the forest timber, that formerly lent such an air of richness and grandeur to the varied landscape, has entirely disappeared.

[15] The oldest stone castle of Blarney is supposed to have been built, in the year 1200, by Mac Carthy, king of South Munster. The present ruinous structure is said to have been raised on its foundation, about the middle of the fifteenth century, by Cormac MacCarthy surnamed Laidhear, or the Strong, who became possessed of his lordship in 1449. The castle and abbey of Kilcrea, the castle of Carricknamuck, the nunnery of Ballyvacadine and five other churches, owe their erection to him. He was wounded at Carricknamuck, he died at Cork, and was interred in Kilcrea Abbey, A. D. 1494. In the beginning of the present century his tomb, bearing a Latin epitaph, might be seen; but it has long since disappeared. This abbey is represented as furnishing the scene of a creditable poetic legend, called the "Monks of Kilcrea," written by an anonymous author, and commencing with these lines:

> "Three monks sat by a bogwood fire,
>   Bare were their crowns, and their garments grey.
> Close sat they to that bogwood fire,
>   Watching the wicket till break of day:
>   Such was ever the rule of Kilcrea."

In the year 1602, the castle of Blarney was in possession of Cormac Mac Dermot Carthy, who was charged with being an accomplice of the Irish forces, then engaged in rebellion against the government of Queen Elizabeth. At this period, the castle was considered one of the largest and strongest fortifications within the province of Munster. In the *Pacata Hibernia*, we are told, that "it is fower piles joyned in one, seated upon a maine rock, so as it is free from myning, the wall eighteene foote thicke, and well flancked, at each corner to the best advantage."—*Chap.* xii. A base plot had been contrived to get possession of this stronghold, but it failed; however, the Irish chieftain was afterwards constrained to surrender his castle to Captain Taaffe, for the queen's service. Blarney remained in possession of the Lords of Muskerry; and during the great insurrection of 1641, it gave very considerable annoyance to the royalist citizens and garrison of Cork, until taken, early in the year 1646, by Lord Broghill, afterwards Earl of Orrery. It was held by the Republican forces from that period, until the Cromwellian war had terminated. Donogh Mac Carthy, Baron of Blarney, was created Viscount Muskerry and Earl of Clancarty by Charles II. in 1658; the greater part of his forfeited estates having been restored by the Act of Settlement. A collateral descendant of his, named also Donough, the fourth earl, obtained command of a troop of Horse Guards, from James II., in 1693, and he afterwards served in the wars of that ill-fated monarch. After the Revolution, the Muskerry estates were again declared forfeited to the crown. In 1701, the castle of Blarney was purchased by Sir James Jeffreys, governor of Cork, who erected a large and handsome residence, adjoining the shattered fortress. This was the family mansion for successive generations; but it has long since become a dilapidated, yet picturesque ruin.

No. IX.

A Legend of Aughrim.

—

THE TAINTED STREAM.

WHERE boomed the cannon, flashed the glaive,
 Along that ridge of green, [1]
Where fought and fell the strong and brave,
Who found in death their blood-stained grave,
 A limpid fount is seen.

But if, 'midst Nubia's parching sands,
 Beneath the camels' feet,
It flowed as bright on those far lands,
The fainting hordes of Arab bands
 Might sink through noon-tide heat,

Ere beast or man would bend beside
 That clear and ripling wave,
To taste the bitter draught, its tide
Pours down those green slopes, spreading wide
 By many a hero's grave. [2]

———

NOTES.

[1] A visit to the battle field of Aughrim is peculiarly interesting,
not alone from the historic reminiscences connected with this spot, but
owing to the wide, extended and varied prospect, presented from the
commanding position of Kilcommedan heights. Tradition maintains,
that the high-crested fences and copse-crowned embankments, sepa-

rating those rich pastures on the eastern slope of the Irish line, remain with little alteration from the period of the 12th of July (old style), 1691, to this present time. The events of that memorable day are on record, and the plan of battle is best illustrated on its ground, by the information and traditions of local residents. A large hawthorn-tree, "with seats beneath the shade," is pointed out on the side of Kilcommedan, where St. Ruth is said to have fallen, and to have been interred, according to some accounts. The ruins of an old castle, that formerly commanded a causeway, by which the right flank of the English army assailed the Irish left, are yet traceable in the village of Aughrim. The position selected for the defeated army was creditable to the judgment of its brave but unfortunate general. However, at the present day, the morasses in front would present few obstacles to the advance of a numerous and disciplined attacking force, led against the ridge of hills, running nearly north-west by south-east, and skirting the village of Aughrim, on towards the pass of Urraghree. The intricate and intersecting hedgerows, with deep ditches, extending along the declivities of the hills, and in front of the Irish battle-lines, formed their most effective defence for the less numerous host, badly paid, equipped and armed, dispirited by previous reverses, weakened by desertions, and filled with distrustful or discordant views, owing to the estrangement and dissension prevailing amongst their leaders. The accident of St. Ruth's death mainly determined the loss of that memorable battle. The first of Erin's bards most probably had the results and scenes of Aughrim present to his imagination, when penning the beautiful national lyric, commencing with these lines:

> " Forget not the field where they perish'd,
> The truest, the last of the brave ;
> All gone—and the bright hope we cherish'd
> Gone with them, and quench'd in their grave !"

[2] On the hill-side, near Kilcommedan, trickles a streamlet, from which cattle are never known to drink. It is said to have flowed with human gore, on the fatal day of the battle fought at Aughrim ; and it is presumed the unnatural tinge then assumed by its waters imparted a bitter taste, which no degree of thirst nor lapse of time can ever render palatable.

No. X.

A Legend of Dunamase.

THE ENCHANTED BANDOG.

When time was young, and hope with mantling smile
Spread promised peace around our sea-girt isle,
When freeborn men preserved in Freedom's fane
Their rule and laws unswayed by foreign thane;
Ere Norse or Saxon waged destructive fight,
Ere monk from Druid held a differing rite,
When the wild forest spread its awful shades
O'er massive cromlechs, sheltering midst its glades,
Ere pillar tower, its head half lost in sky,
Looked over hill and dale, so hoar and high,
No castle-turret crown'd the solid base,
That props thy present ruins, Dunamase!

Thy frowning rock was then a chosen seat
Of peaceful men, in war their last retreat,
For vain th' assailant's might, and weak his sword,
Drawn 'gainst the foe, that stood its summit's lord,
Who dared such combat from beneath, his life
Paid forfeit for rash courage in that strife.

Then Normans came. The mail-clad baron bold,
And armed vassals pitched their feudal hold
Upon the eyrie steep; they girt it round

With many a flanking tower, with moat and mou
Embrasured turrets, proud and grimly set,
Rear'd o'er the beetling heights their coronet.
Even yet are seen, to mock the rage of man,
That dismal dungeon, wardroom, barbican.
The massive keep, with roofless walls of grey,
Shall sternly rise through many a future day.·

'Twas rumoured long, that in this mid-air hold,
Reward of war and rapine, hoarded gold
Lay buried deep, and lies ; but how or where
To gain the prize, few know, or knowing dare,
For awful tales the villagers affright,
Of visions erst revealed to mortal sight. [1]

'Tis said that dreams of Erebus [2] are born,
And issue forth, through ivory gates, or horn : [3]
But true or false, what wond'rous fancies spring,
Midst the tranc'd slumbers, nightly visions bring.
In fitful starts, through Michaul's troubled sleep,
Thrice airy visions passed in playful sweep. [4]
He views a cumbrous ledge, the wall below—
An arching stone uprais'd—a shining row
Of golden ingots piled beneath a stone
Surpassing strength of man to raise alone !
He wakes—he doubts—yet doubting, he decides
What course to take : that secret he confides
To chosen friends, who credulous as he,
Would try the issue, numbering only three,
Resolved to quest their fortune, when the light ‑
Of parting day gave place to sable night.

With eager hope, yet dashed by craven fear,
Forth sped the trio, till in sight appear,
Those dusky ruins, towering on high,
With outlines looming, drawn across the sky.
Beneath the shattered arches of each wall
Their falt'ring steps, with measured echoes fall,
Whilst from the hollow'd chinks and crannies fly
Scared bats and owlets, with a piercing cry.

The mattock rings at length, the levers groan,
Beneath a jutting mass of basement stone :
Full many a heave and nervous blow bestowed
Relieved with painful toil th' incumbent load,
Whilst loosen'd rocks are piled in heaps around
A mimic cavern yawned beneath the ground.
Then, joy of joys ! the covering arch-stone bares
Its massive surface, and the band prepares,
With wild excitement gleaming from tranc'd eyes,
To lift the pond'rous seal, and gain their prize !

Well poised, the crowbars tug with labouring strain,
The flag is rocked below, yet rocked in vain.
Such fruitless efforts plied, mattock and spade
Must delve around the base : till openings made
Beneath the stone require these stalwart men
To urge their iron levers' power again.
With pinch well set and groaning weight, that block
Of massive shape upheaved divides the rock !

What sight appears ! Lo, golden piles were there !
Each toil-worn wight gloats o'er his equal share,

And instant visions of the future rise,
In misty shapes before their dazzled eyes,
Proud mansions, titles, wealth, with broad domains,
Rule unconfin'd, o'er far extending plains !

Hark, what a growl ! it rumbles from beneath !
Hush'd are admiring words, and still'd each breath !
Fork'd lightning gleams around in spreading sheet,
The quaking rock is mov'd beneath their feet !
A sulph'rous smell, with clouds of blinding smoke
In thick'ning wreaths from out the cavern broke.
High crumbling walls from summit to their base
Seem topling down the sides of Dunamase.
Nor direr discord girded it of yore,
When sped the vivid flash and cannon's roar ;
When banded forces urged with fell alarms
Their hostile engines and opposing arms :
Through midnight's loneliness, above, around,
Convulsive shocks and hollow thunders sound.
With shaggy locks, that bristle like to spears,
And opening jaws, a monster mastiff rears ;
His fearful teeth are set with venom'd ire,
His flashing eye-balls roll a stream of fire,
Forth from that cave he springs, where long he lay,
And pour'd on stilly night a hoarse loud bay.
Not half so fierce or hideous, he that sate
The fabled ward of Pluto's lower gate. [5]

Enough to tempt such danger, who could stand
The shock of fear that shook our peasant band ?
Farewell to golden visions, hopeful dreams !

Cold dew-drops wet their brows, unmanly screams
Are borne upon the echoes of that night,
As heedless fall their steps in hastening flight.
With nimble bound, with shelving rocks before,
And wildering looks, they leaped these ledges o'er,
Nor durst they turn a glance to visions fear'd
Till moat and mound and fence were lightly clear'd,
Till sights and sounds recede from eyes and ears,
And distance gave interval to their fears.

The waning night, with canopy of cloud,
O'er slumbering nature spread her dusky shroud,
And dimly curtained distant Dunamase,
Its frowning towers, rocks, and neighbouring chase. [6]
Whilst stillness slept around the beechen trees, [7]
No breath of air e'en stirred a passing breeze.
Then, gathering close, with beating hearts, our three
Redoubted heroes breathe a moment free,
First cast their furtive glances round, and then
One straining look; but never thought again
Within their craven bosoms faintly beat,
To risk once more like danger and defeat.
Turning to seek their homes that fearful night,
With downcast spirits and in piteous plight,
All former dread departs as float the grey
Cold morning mists before the solar ray.
But ere they separate, each shame-faced wight
Gave pledge to guard all secrets of that night.

" A secret keeps with one, but not with two :"
So saith the proverb—in this case prov'd true—

A pari reasoning, scarcely leaves a doubt,   ·
That three must surely leak such secret out.
This tale though told in prose full many a time,
Yet vainly sought its bardic shape in rhyme ;
Of local fame, tradition-borne along,
None deemed it worth the guerdon of a song ;
Whilst earth is searched for themes to twine full bays
Round laureate brows, in epics, odes or lays,
Might not a rustic muse, new-string her lyre
And chant to son the fictions of his sire ?
Old scenes, old customs, olden time and tale
Like sun gone down, each instant fading pale,
Like music's notes suspended, still the strain
Wakes in the ear or mind, so sweet again,
We prize yet more the parting tones and light,
When harp-strings rest, and gloom leads on to night :
So ere the past be unregenerate, gone,
Seize on some traits that waft its features on,
And let the modern minstrel still rehearse,
Whate'er may grace, whate'er adorn his verse.
Green Erin ! thine be tributary song,
May patriot bards their fame and thine prolong,
And frame grey legends, as through ancient days,
Tuneful to numbers in their roundelays.

NOTES.

[1] The subject matter of this legend, I have heard related by
the sister of the dreamer and principal actor here introduced. Him I ·
once knew, as a comfortable and respected small farmer, living in the
immediate neighbourhood of Dunamase rock and castle, near the

town of Maryborough. In my younger days, having paid many a
visit to this celebrated and romantic spot, whilst lingering often
amongst these extensive feudal ruins, I was shown certain excavations
in various places around the massive walls and near their foundations.
These diggings were said to have been executed by nocturnal money-
hunters. I never recollect hearing, however, whether any of their
explorations proved successful; although I have been told of many
persons, who from humble positions attained to a respectable inde-
pendence, owing to their fortunate acquisition of money, found in or
near old castles, houses, raths or antiquated erections. About thirty
years have elapsed since the following reported occurrences took place,
near the old church and grave-yard of Kilteale, lying quite contiguous
to the rock of Dunamase. A farmer, named Whelan, dreamed that
money was buried at a certain spot, within the embankment of an
old rath, covered with hawthorn, and which formed a part of his
holding. To this nightly vision little import was then attached.
Being superior in intelligence to, and above the prevailing prejudices
and superstitions of, his class, notwithstanding dissuasions and sinister
warnings from his neighbours, this man afterwards resolved on levelling
the rath, thus increasing the area of a field for cultivation. Whilst
engaged on this work, and near the very spot to which his dream referred, he actually displaced an antique earthen vessel, filled with many
curious silver coins. These he sold, as I have been informed, to his
landlord, the late Captain Baldwin of Raheenduff House, near
Stradbally. On the townland of Ballymaddock, adjoining Kilteale,
whilst labourers were engaged in removing a hedge-row, the perfect
skeleton of some person, who had probably met with a violent end
many years back and had been there concealed, was found. No tradition remained, to account satisfactorily for the nature of this singular interment, independently of the circumstance that led to such accidental discovery. The older inhabitants of the neighbourhood,
however, recollected that this lonely district was the noted haunt of
outlaws and robbers, whose deeds of rapine were probably attended on
occasions with the sacrifice of human life. One of these desperadoes
was captured, after an exciting chase, by the Captain Baldwin, already
alluded to; yet, not without imminent risk, and a desperate attempt

made to murder the gallant gentleman, who successfully accomplished this daring feat.

[2] Erebus, the mythologic impersonation of Darkness, was the son of Chaos and Nox, and father of the day. Erebus denoted the gloomy region, distinguished from Tartarus, the place of torments, and from Elysium, the region of felicity. According to Virgil's account, Erebus comprised several districts, in which the shades of departed persons underwent peculiar expiations.

[3]   "Sunt geminae somni portae : quarum altera fertur
       Cornea, qua veris facilis datur exitus umbris :
       Altera candenti perfecta nitens elephanto ;
       Sed falsos ad coelum mittunt in somnia Manes."

                                 Ænidos.   *Lib.* vi.

[4] The theory of dreams, as interpreted in Ireland, is rather complicated and contradictory in application. No superstition is more general, however, than a belief in the verification of a dream thrice repeated on successive nights, especially when referring—as it usually does—to the concealment of treasure in some particular spot. As the course of true love seldom runs smooth, so, search or hazard, in a pursuit of vision-pictured riches, rarely eventuates in a successful issue or rewards the excited hopes of our imaginative peasantry.

[5] The following lines, descriptive of Cerberus, are found in Hesiod :

     " Δουτερον αὖτις ἔτικτεν ἀμήχανον, ουτι φατειὸν,
       Κέρβερον ὠμηστην, 'Αἴδεω κύνα χαλκεόφωνον,
       Πεντηκοντακάρηνον, ἀναιδέα τε κρατερόν τε."

                          ΘΕΟΓΟΝΙΑ.   *vv.* 310, 311, 312.

[6] The park or chase of this remarkable feudal fortress extended towards the west, and lay immediately under frowning summits of limestone rock. Some traces of a walled enclosure may still be seen, and also several copsewood thickets, on rugged eminences, within this boundary.

[7] When the property of Dunamase rock and castle pertained to the Parnell family, a fine grove of beech trees, beneath the crags, added very considerably to scenic effect, even within the writer's me-

mory. These sylvan ornaments have been removed. It is said the woods surrounding this seat of mediæval grandeur afforded convenient haunts for outlaws and nocturnal depredators, during the disturbed period of 1832 and 1833, when this district was under the operation of martial law. This is one of the principal causes assigned for their disappearance. The remains of trenches, thrown up by the parliamentarian forces, under Colonels Hewson and Reynolds in 1650, may be seen on an opposite hill, which is separated, by a deep valley, from the rock and its dilapidated fortifications. To these several objects will suitably apply the lines of Tasso, in his description of that peculiar situation, occupied by the Holy City,

> " sovra due colli è posta
> D'impári altezza, e volti fronte a fronte.
> Va per lo mezzo suo valle interposta,
> Che lei distingue, e l'un dall' altro monte.
> Fuor da tre lati ha malagevol costa :
> Per l'altro vassi, e non par che si monte :
> Ma d'altissime mura à più difesa
> La parte plana, e 'ncontra Borea stesa."
>
> *Gerusalemme Liberata.* Canto iii. ; stanza lv.

Resting on the parapet of these entrenchments, the eye is carried by a direct line, on a level, to the keep and upper defensive works of Dunamase castle. From this position, the Cromwellian batteries played with destructive effect on its fortifications. On the green sward, within the outer defences of Dunamase, I recollect having seen the deeply indented traces of foot-marks, in which the O'Mores are said to have stood, when engaged practising in pairs, at sword exercises.

No. XI.

A Legend of Holy Cross Abbey.

THE CULDEE VISION.

WHEN mellowed hues at evening's close spread o'er the
distant meadows,
  And on Slieve Felim's mountain top, [1] the sunlight
  fades from view,
When furtive creeps the gathering haze of mystic wreathed
shadows,
  Like diamonds shine the earlier stars, that spangle heaven's blue.
Oft may the pensive wanderer, beside each moulded arch
  That props the ruined abbey walls, [2] with buttresses
  so grey,
List to the magic prelude notes, as forth in solemn
march,
  Long trains of spectral churchmen move unseen, at
  close of day.

The massive turret stands as yet, where ravens find their
home,
  And ivy clings around its walls, the river murmurs by;
The nave though roofless screens a choir, not altarless become,
  Amidst tall trees, the lightest breeze most musical doth
  sigh :

When swells that choral anthem, with tower-bells loud
    pealing,
  Sweet *carrillons* [8] adown the vales slow lingering chime
    and last,
Then may the mind, through fancy's maze, touch every
    chord of feeling,
  And bring from olden times remote some echoes of the
    past.

Man hath a mission of his own, and at a distant time
  Must yet redeem the rapine made upon this noble fane.
One, whose broad lands and golden hoard may fittingly
    combine
  To rescue from their ruined state those fragments that
    remain,
Shall feel inspired again to raise a pent-roof o'er those
    aisles,
  And rest the spandril joists against the gables' pointed
    walls ; [4]
Again the pattering brumal rain may drip adown the tiles,
  And sunbeams pass through coloured glass, o'er richly
    fashioned stalls.

Then, once again, the Culdee [5] strain shall rise at early
    morning ;
  The Matin strophe and antistrophe, the Lauds, with
    psalm and hymn,
Shall roll in cadence grand and sweet from floor to oak-
    ribbed awning ;
  At intervals of forenoon shall the chapter hours begin.

Then surpliced *frères*, in ordered ranks, at evening shall
    entone
    Their vesper song and complin psalm, when sinks the
        setting sun,
And whilst the pendant midnight lamp lights aisles so dim
    and lone,
    Their eyes shall close, in blest repose, toil, prayer and
        vigil done.

Whilst song and prayer, in upper air, as if from Angel
    bands,
    Pour down in holiest harmonies rejoicings of the blest,
A grand refrain, must wake again, o'er wide and fertile
    lands,
    Strains plaintive, 'slow and solemn, whilst the sons of
        labour rest.
But like that dazzling brightness, when the sheeted light-
    nings glance
    Athwart the midnight gloom, but with mild effulgent
        gleam,
The distant canopy illumed, while 'midst the light advance
    Those monks of yore, unseen before, now clear as noon-
        tide beam.

Around the concave vault of blue, stars paling with a
    dightness
    Of rays celestial, halos crown those habitants of bliss;
And years may speed the course of time, ere visions of
    such brightness
    Will cease to pour from spirit world its glorious sheen
        on this.

Until the patron lord shall reach his span of life decreed,
  And Heaven recalls the pilgrim to that brighter, better
    goal,
Which cares foreclose, ambitious aims, when happily suc-
    ceed
  Those fadeless joys, saints raptured deem true pleasures
    of the soul.

One summer night, in robes of white, whilst mortals still
    repose,
  That Culdee train of spirits blest shall throng around
    his grave ;
And heard again, one requiem strain, such tones for ever
    close
  From upper air to human ears.   Yet still within the
    nave,
The aisles and choir, so well restored, so loved and che-
    rished long,
  In cloistered life, to distant age, those brethren of that
    school,
At stated times shall sweetly chant their mass and sacred
    song,
  Regarding well their chastening vows, their rubric and
    their rule.

NOTES.

[1] The Slievefelim mountains lie in the north-eastern corner of
the county of Limerick, adjoining the county of Tipperary.   Cullaun,
the highest point, rises 1,523 feet over the ocean level.   Separated by
a deep pass, the still more elevated Mauher-Slieve, or Mother Moun-

tain, extends in a north-easterly direction, and bending thence along
the western borders of Tipperary, various heights look over the fertile
Golden Vale, through which the river Suir winds.   Many objects of
curious antiquarian interest will be found within this district; and
amongst other noted places may be enumerated the grave of Emona-
knock, Dermod and Grania's bed, Rathnacloghgal fort and Laght-
seefin.   The latter lies between the copper mines near Knockbane
and the waterfall of Poulanass on Aughnaglanny river.

[2] Allusion is here made to the celebrated Abbey of Holy Cross,
situated on the western bank of the Suir river, a few miles from
Thurles.   The ruins are highly picturesque and of imposing extent.
Immediately near the village an ancient bridge of several arches spans
the river.   Holy Cross Abbey is said to have derived its denomination,
from the circumstance of having been built and endowed with lands
by Donogh Carbragh O'Brian, king of Thomond, in 1182, to serve as
the depositary for a relic of the true Cross, which had been obtained
from Rome.   I have been informed, that this precious relic is even
yet preserved by a parish priest, in an adjoining diocese.   The abbey
belonged to the Cistercians, and its superior formerly took his place
in Parliament, as a mitred abbot, with the title Earl of Holy Cross.
The principal building was of cruciform shape, having a square
tower in the centre.   A nave, chancel and transept diverged from
this point.   Two beautifully groined chapels may be seen on the
south side of the choir.   A double row of Gothic arches, supported
by twisted black marble pillars, lies between these chapels.   According to an old tradition, the monks were waked under the canopied
niche here formed: other accounts say that the relic of the true Cross
was deposited in this place.   Two other chapels may be observed on
the northern side of the choir.   The towers and chapels are highly
finished in an architectural point of view; whilst the coved roof and
arches are elegantly ribbed and moulded with a superior quality of
limestone.   The ancient cloisters, extending round a large quadrangular grass plot, are ruinous, but highly interesting.   Several of the
old tombs within the enclosure are sadly disfigured; the former inscrip-
tions are obliterated in many instances, and covered over with modern
epitaphs.   The late very learned, amiable and accomplished parish

priest of Clonoulty, the Rev. Thomas O'Carroll, had been long engaged on a historical work, referring to Holy Cross Abbey : it is to be hoped that this literary production may yet be published. In Grose's *Antiquities of Ireland*, vol. i., will be found three large copperplate engravings, representing the interior, the exterior, and a ground-plan of this abbey, before the close of the last century.

[3] The musical toned measure and accord of bells in church and cåthedral turrets.

[4] The people living in immediate contiguity to Holy Cross Abbey entertain an idea, that at some remote period, this religious establishment will be restored to its original purposes by the lord of the manor, and that it will so continue to the end of time. Certain proposals, I have been informed, were actually made by its Protestant proprietor, at no distant period, to have it restored for purposes of Catholic worship, but the expenses necessary to be incurred were deemed too great for prudential considerations, in reference to this matter. To the gentleman in question, every admirer of antiquarian taste in objects of ancient architectural art must feel indebted, for a correct although partial effort to preserve Holy Cross Abbey from the slow, wasting process of ruin and decay. Several of the sculptured stones have been reset at his expense; some of the broken mullioned windows have been cramped with iron, or repaired ; and the whole of the interior enclosed has been consigned to the charge of a resident caretaker.

[5] The term céjle bé, Anglicised *Culdee*, is used by our annalists to denote a monk or friar, even at a comparatively modern period of our history. In O'Donovan's *Annals of the Four Masters*, at the year 1595, we find an application of such term to the Dominicans in Sligo monastery. The reader, who desires the fullest accumulated testimonies and learned investigation, in reference to the Culdees, will examine the researchful contribution of the Rev. William Reeves, in *Transactions of the Royal Irish Academy*, vol. xxiv. It has since been published as a separate tract, entitled, *The Culdees of the British Islands, as they appear in History, with an Appendix of Evidences*: Dublin, 1864.

No. XII.

A Legend of Lough Erne.

THE PIESTHA.

GLIDE round those softest shores and isles
O'er which the orb of heaven smiles
    On sweet Lough Erne, [1]
And ask, if in this world of ours
More past'ral beauty richly dowers
    Fair scenes and stern.

'Midst Nature's dimpled, winning charms
Should craftsmen dream of dread alarms
    Buoyed on its breast,
When earnest peering through the wave,
They feel and see the Peistha [2] heave
    With ponderous crest ?

Large as the Kraken's [3] monstrous form
When riding through the wintry storm
    Near Norway's coast ;
Long trailing as the ocean eel, [4]
His curving course Erne's waves reveal
    When tempest tost.

Or when the flood is bright and calm
With summer's breath distilling balm
    From odorous brakes,

Till clustering isles the view debar,
A glassy surface glows afar
    Within those lakes.

From wooded Crom [5] to Inisbrath [6]
The Peistha wends his devious path
    Naan Castle [7] round,
By Inishleague [8] and green Belleisle [9]
Oft doth the dusky monster steal
    Low through the sound.

To stately Enniskillen town
Beneath its bridge still gliding down
    By Laisre's fane, [10]
By Trasna, Car and Ferney shore, [11]
Dacharne, [12] Macsaint [13] and Lustymore [14]
    He turns again :

And breasts the current's upward course
With floating fins and sturdy force
    Then sinks eftsoons ;
And well the waterman may fear
To check the creature's slow career
    In deep lagoons.

Cold lie his limbs beneath the wave,
Uncoffined in an early grave
    And noteless tomb :
Let cautious cruisers then beware,
Lest skimming o'er Lough Erne they share
    Such fatal doom. [15]

NOTES.

[1] The celebrated and beautiful Lough Erne, studded over with more than two hundred islands—some of these being of very considerable extent—flows in a north-west course, almost centrally through the county of Fermanagh. It is supplied with many tributary streams, along the forty miles of its tortuous channel; being divided into the upper and lower lake. About midway on an island in the Erne, the elegantly built and thriving town of Enniskillen stands, two handsome bridges, having five arches each, connecting this borough with the mainland. The romantic scenery both above and below this town is unrivalled. The upper lake has numerous indentations along its margin on either side, and so thickly are its islands grouped, that at first sight it would seem a matter of extreme difficulty for a pilot to find the proper channel. It gives the tourist a general idea of an inundated country. The islands are usually very fertile and verdant, whilst many are richly wooded. Projecting headlands on the river banks are sometimes covered with fine timber, rising with stately trunks and branching tops from the low and often marshy grounds. Herons and aquatic fowl breed along the rush-lined shores. Nothing can exceed the variety of landscape features here introduced. Swelling hills and more distant mountains frequently give a grand, undulating outline to the prospect. The lower lake has a greater expansion of water, unimpeded by islands; although the latter are found to be not less numerous, when descending its stream. Bo or Cow Island is the largest on the lower lake, and affords most excellent pasturage. In the summer season, a well appointed steamer plies along the most interesting part of Lough Erne, and is found most convenient for tourist purposes.

[2] The *Peistha* is a sort of immense Dragon or Water Serpent which lies enchanted at the bottom of nearly all the lakes of Ireland. That fabled monster, lying under the waters of Lough Erne, is supposed to continue its upward and downward course, without taking rest, until the day of judgment. In few instances does the huge animal appear above the surface, and only whilst heavy wreaths of foam curl over the lake, when storms prevail

[3] A supposititious sea-animal of amazing dimensions. If we credit the account given by Bishop Pontoppidan, in his Natural History of Norway, its back or upper part seems an English mile and a-half in circumference, whilst it is covered with rugged excrescences. The Kraken is supposed to be of crab-like shape, and to rise or swim only over very deep soundings.

[4] Mariners have given us, at various times, some very extraordinary statements, regarding this creature. It is said to be of immense thickness and length, having a mane surmounting the back and waving as it advances through the water. Naturalists, however, have not been able to afford any very positive evidence, as to the existence of such a wonderful marine monstrosity.

[5] The magnificent trees, extending around Crom Castle and grouped over its fine demesne, are nearly altogether closed in by the embayed waters of Lough Erne.

[6] A finely timbered but small island in the upper lake.

[7] The site of Naan Castle lies on the western shore of a green, unwooded island, bearing the same denomination.

[8] Inishleage lies near the former isle, and is partially wooded.

[9] When residents in the fine mansion on this exquisitely improved island, the Earl and Countess of Rosse effected, by judicious combinations, fine artificial effects to increase the natural features of its scenery. An elegant bridge connects this island, formerly called Bally-Mac-Manus, with the eastern shore. Killygowan and Inishreagh, adjoining Islands, are also delightfully planted with trees. All of these are included within the parish of Derrybrusk.

[10] St. Laisre, also called St. Laserian, Molaisse or Molush, is said to have founded a religious establishment on the Island of Devenish, at the entrance to lower Lough Erne, in the sixth century. Subsequent additions were made about the middle of the fifteenth century, when a priory was founded. A very interesting group of monastic ruins is here surmounted by a round tower, built of a light brown sandstone, found in the neighbourhood. This island of Devenish is remarkable for its extraordinary fertility.

[11] These three verdant islands, lying below Devenish, are denuded of trees.

[12] Dacharne and all its surrounding headlands are covered with noble, luxuriant woods, and they present probably the most admired points of view on lower Lough Erne.

[13] Inishmacsaint, which is fringed with trees on its northern margin, contains a ruined church and a favourite burial-ground : it is also situated on the lower Lough, near Ross Point. Most enchanting views are presented on every side, as the voyager moves down towards the widest spreading water of the Erne, before it becomes contracted, above Belleek.

[14] Lustymore and Lustybeg Islands lie conterminous, southward of Bo Island. They are covered over with fine forest trees. Highly picturesque effects are produced by the reflection of various islands and their foliage on the surface of Lough Erne, when the waters are still and whilst the atmosphere is perfectly clear.

[15] There is another superstition prevailing in various parts of Ireland, and similar in many respects to the preceding legend. A *sea-horse* is said to lie at the bottom of certain fresh water loughs or sometimes under the ocean. Its apparition is supposed to be fatal to the individual by whom he is encountered. In Scotland, also, the *kelpie* is a supposed spirit of the waters, under the shape of a horse. There is likewise the story told in Ireland of a monster, somewhat similar in many of its properties to the foregoing animals. It is called the *master-otter*, a portion of whose skin, possessed by any individual, will render his house fire-proof and preserve himself safe from any evil results of shipwreck, steel or bullet.

No. XIII.

A Legend of Murrisk.

THE DULLAHAN.

GRANDLY and desolate stretch those mountains high,
That piled irregularly skirt fair shores,
Their varied cones extending far through space ;
And over all Croagh Patrick's [1] towering peak,
Surmounted by its ruined, hollowed cell,
Where pilgrims oft resort with toilsome steps
To offer vows and prayers at the rude shrine,
Once blessed by him, whose living presence breathed
A balmy fragrance fresh to after time.
When the wild storm careers on those bare heights,
And ocean's drifting mists hang round their sides,
How solitarily stern the landward range
Of vasty undulations, bleak and sear,
With stony ridges, through a wilderness,
Where gurgle down from moor and sedgy marsh
In rushing torrents turbid mountain streams.
But still more lonesome, when the rowan, oak,
Or rooted brake and briar covered o'er
Those vales and steeps with growth indigenous,
A covert for the deer or prowling wolves,
Or forming grateful shades for feathered choirs
That warble thrilling wood-notes through the spring.

When silent midnight reigns around the coast,
Whilst hoarsely surging billows beat that strand.

The lonely walls of Murrisk [2] rise beside
And many a grave lies near, where still repose
Whole generations of the dead.   Cold gleams
The dubious light or shade, which flickers o'er
That sad receptacle of human forms.
When like some troubled spirit of the deep,
The fisher's broad sail swells along its brine,
And yeasty foams the ocean in his wake,
The salt spray dashing from a cleaving prow.
Perchance the watching mariner looks through
A waste of seething waves, as billows roll.
He scans the distant shore with eager eye
To catch the gleam of faggot in his hut,
Where wife and children, dear to his fond heart,
Expect the wanderer home, this starlit hour,
Or rest in calm repose, till near the beach
His loaded smack be moored in its safe cove.

From out the walls of Murrisk, sudden heard,
A sound as if from cannon booming thence,
With frequent crashes followed, when along
The *Coach-a-bower*, drawn by headless steeds
Went bounding o'er the sea-side road apace.
Two flashing lamps threw light to either fence
And upwards, till the welkin bright illumed
Revealed this portent to the fisher's gaze.
The headless coachman lashed his foaming steeds,
And crouched within, but wrapped in gloom, appears
Some lordly magnate, on his couch reclined;
Yet whether lounging in luxurious ease,
As Dives in his life-time pleasure loved,

Or suffering much in state, for thus he seemed,
How vainly could mere mortal speculate.

Not long that level road the rolling wheels
Indented, till a *bohar's* [8] opening reached,
The plunging horses dashed with furious pace
Through its intricacies : for never yet
Had chariot of the rudest fashion passed
Within that deep ravine by current worn.
But strangest sight of all ! high up the steep
The lumbering equipage ascending still,
Like some dark hearse on destined errand bound
Above Croagh Patrick's reek.   One moment stood
The Dullahan, [4] then down the rockly cone
Where'er the rapid chariot wheels revolved
Fell boulders rudely swept from their loose bed.
Along the rugged tops of mountains bare
Swift moved the headless roadsters on their course,
Taking full circuit of the blasted heath
And rumbling over numerous mountain streams
Deep sunk within their dells, once more regained
The causeway broad.   Within a narrow lane
That chariot rolled, and lost to vision soon
Hid by the abbey walls, which echoing loud
Prolonged reverberation round the shores.

Appalled the fisher gazed, till through the gloom
A sight more awful tranced his soul with dread,
For through the darkness rose one burst of flame
Which shot with lambent energy above

The humble home that sheltered those he loved.
The mountain heath, which thatched his cabin roof,
Flung radiance far, whilst blazing high in air.
Alas ! what anguish wrung the sailor's breast
In sad uncertainty to learn the fate
Of his fond wife and children, hopeful still,
Life had been spared and future time might bring
In double measure heaped his perished store.
Impatient, yet divining ills to bear,
Demanding years of toil on sea and shore,
The laggard breezes bore him o'er the waves.

When daylight dawned his bark had touched the strand,
And groups of villagers surround the spot,
Fearing to breathe those messages of woe
Which bursting sighs and tears might best reveal.
Yet to the husband's agonized demand,
And wringing more the suppliant father's heart,
'Twas told, that piercing shrieks of wife and child
Were heard convulsive 'midst the rushing flame
Till all was still : and when the morning came
Black charred remains were found beneath a pile
Of smoking embers.   Sad was the closing scene !
To Murrisk grave-yard moved a sorrowing train,
Seven coffins ranged beside rest 'neath the sod,
And woe-distraught, the weeping fisher bent
Wailing the live-long night, till stark and cold,
Refusing aid or comfort, stretched he lay
A corpse upon the new-made graves.   The earth
Claimed its last tenant, under Murrisk walls,

Which stand above that row of hapless dead,
Whilst near with dirge-like cadence beat the waves
In moaning surges on a lonely shore.

NOTES.

[1] The lofty summit of Croagh Patrick rises 2,510 feet over the ocean level. The upper cone is very steep. In the month of August, 1860, having been accompanied on a short tour through this part of Connaught, by my dear friend the Rev. Ulick J. Bourke, Professor of Irish, in St. Jarlath's College, Tuam, after a toilsome ascent, occupying two full hours without rest or intermission, we were enabled to reach the rude cell on its very summit, in which St. Patrick is said to have fasted and prayed during a whole Lent. It is hollowed in the rock, and built up round the sides with large, rude stones. The rushing winds that played round this upper region were piercingly cold and loaded with vapour, which in the shape of white, misty clouds frequently rested on the mountain sides, intercepting a vast range of prospect. These obstructions occasionally cleared off, and then the view was one of unrivalled sublimity. Towards the south, dark mountain tops and deep valleys were everywhere extended; and towards the ocean, a land-locked bay was studded over with a multitude of islands. Lying outwards, like giant fortresses to guard the harbour entrance, that field of vision reached far

" by distant Erris' side,
" Where Clare's tall cliffs opposed the dashing sea."

Notwithstanding our uncomfortable position, comparative shelter had been afforded by the ruined oratory, and we remained for some time, lost in admiration of the wild, magnificent scenery, beneath and around us. Tradition asserts, as Ned Lysaght has sung, that from the top of this mountain,

" At St. Patrick's command,
Vipers quitted the land,"

and disappeared in the wide-spreading bay, near Westport. Croagh

Patrick is a celebrated resort for pilgrims, who assemble there from even distant parts, and recite certain prayers, at various "stations," on its summit.

[2] The ruins of Murrisk Abbey are situated about five miles from Westport, on the southern shore of Clew Bay, with its hundred islands, and immediately at the foot of the towering Croagh Patrick. A very excellent engraving, from an original drawing by Bigari, in the Right Hon. William Conyngham's collection, may be seen in Grose's *Antiquities of Ireland*, vol. i. p. 41. The old walls are yet tolerably well preserved, although in a very exposed situation. This abbey formerly belonged to Eremites of the Augustinian order, and was founded by the O'Mallys.

[3] A *bohar*, in Irish written boṫaṅ, is the name generally used for a road or passage.

[4] The Dullahan, Dulachan, Dubhlachan or Durrachan, are names indiscriminately applied to Irish hobgoblins, represented as appearing without heads. The etymology of the word appears referable to a dark, angry, sullen, fierce or malicious being. Headless apparitions of horses and coachmen are often seen driving from or towards grave-yards, during the dead hour of midnight. Such appearances, where found passing round a particular house, are regarded as ominous of some approaching disaster, and generally indicate a death warning to some member of the family. A deceased nobleman or gentleman is generally supposed to ride within the coach, and the fearful spectacle symbolizes the wanderings of a perturbed spirit, to the excited imagination of the Irish peasant. Headless coachmen, horses and coaches covered with funeral trappings, are usually heard and seen by some solitary watcher, when passing through or looking out on the deserted street of a country town or village. These spectres are often found passing near the spot, where some murder had been committed, or where a fatal accident had happened. The Death-coach receives the name *Coach-a-bower*, in Irish. The heads of men and horses are sometimes seen completely detached from the corresponding bodies. Oftentimes these heads alone are observed flying through the air. Headless horsemen are also seen, and these goblins occasionally carry their heads under their arms, or put them into their pockets. What

seems most surprising, the head is known to speak, although detached from the body.   Yet, the gloomy human apparition, for the
most part moves along, preserving a death-like silence, the coach-
wheels and well shod horses "rattling o'er the stony street."   A loud
cracking of the whip is usually heard, when the headless coachman
drives his preternatural team on the destined course.   I believe
this superstition, regarding the Dullahan, is one that generally prevailed in nearly all those localities, where old charnel-vaults or places
of interment were to be found, and in which some reputedly wicked
member of an aristocratic family had been buried.   If the place happened to be lonely and the old ivied ruin dark and desolate looking,
the accidental sight of an ordinary coach and outriders returning
homewards, during the gloom of midnight, may have contributed, in
many instances, to originate or perpetuate such strange notions
amongst our peasantry.   Similar opinions appear to have prevailed in
other European countries.   But from the peculiarly appalling nature
of this apparition, engrafted amongst our Irish superstitions, I am
inclined to think, it is of northern or Gothic origin ; for in the Eddas
and Sagas of the Northmen, almost every page is filled with allusions
to horror-inspiring fictions, corresponding in characteristics with the
imaginative creations of a rude and unrefined race of people.

No. XIV.

A Legend of Saggard Hill.

THE FAIRY FRIEND'S WARNING.

In slumber deep,
A youth, his sleep
Prolonged beneath the summer skies;
On Saggard Hill [1]
He rested, till
A voice resounded, " Owen, rise !" [2]

He wakes with fear
These sounds to hear,
Prepares to move, but vainly tries;
For o'er his frame
Soft languor came,
Yet, still the voice cried, " Owen, rise !"

His slumber broke,
Again he woke,
And sleep once more sealed o'er his eyes,
Whilst yet the sound
Re-echoed round
The mountain slopes, " Rise, Owen, rise !"

Aroused he leaps
Descending steeps,

His feet scarce track the course he flies,
    But as they press
    He turns to bless
The warning cry of " Owen, rise !" [3]

NOTES.

[1] Saggard Hill must be tolerably familiar to the holiday tourists of our Irish capital. Forming the flank projection of a picturesque defile, it slopes gently along the northern declivities of the Dublin mountains, and contrasts its rich verdure with dunner shades of the more distant over-topping highlands. The visitor, taking his stand on its summit, or driving along the terraced road leading from it to Tallaght, is presented with a magnificent panoramic prospect of the metropolis, the promontory of Howth, the harbour of Dublin, the rich vales of Anna Liffy, and a boundless horizon, beyond the pleasant and fertile plains of Meath. An aspect of wildness—almost of desertion—appears around the mountains in this district, and is rendered the more remarkable, as occurring in the immediate vicinity of a populous city.

[2] The peasantry believe, that few of their families are without some friends in the fairy hosts, and that these familiars often convey a timely warning on the approach of danger. Such admonitions are intended, for the most part, to remove the known effect of intended spells, which might prove disastrous in their consequences. These friendly intimations either prevent the dreaded *blast*, disease, or a future capture and seclusion, within invisible realms,

> " Full of strange shapes, of habits, and of forms,
>   Varying in subjects as the eye doth roll
>   To every varied object in his glance."

[3] The incident versified in this present legend was related to the writer, as having occurred about the middle of the last century, in case of a little boy, who afterwards lived to a very advanced

age. He never ceased to retain a vivid impression of this friendly warning, even in his declining years, and always attributed his preservation from malignant fairy influence, to a guardian spirit, dwelling amongst the mythic tribes. It is also a common belief, that abducted persons, amongst the fairies, often contrive very ingenious expedients to communicate intelligence to their friends on earth. J. J. Callanan has translated into exquisite English verse the Irish song of *Cusheen Loo*, supposed to have been sung by a young bride, who, involuntarily, had

> "winged her journey towards blithe Fairy-land,"

and who had been imprisoned in an elfin fort. Having seen a young female of her acquaintance, near the outside margin, this enchanted woman requested that her husband should be informed about her condition, so that he might bring a steel knife to dissolve the charm, with a flash of its magic blade. On pretence of hushing her infant to sleep, the bride thus sings :

> " Sleep, my child ! for the rustling trees
> Stirred by the breath of summer breeze,
> And fairy songs of sweetest note
> Around us gently float.

> " Sleep ! for the weeping flowers have shed
> Their fragrant tears upon thy head,
> The voice of love hath sooth'd thy rest,
> And thy pillow is a mother's breast.
>   Sleep, my child !"

No. XV.

𝔄 𝔏𝔢𝔤𝔢𝔫𝔡 𝔬𝔣 𝔅𝔩𝔞𝔠𝔨𝔯𝔬𝔠𝔨.

———

THE DISTANT DIRGE.

PROUD castle turrets beetling rise
　　Above the lower Islands,
To deck the Lee in stately guise,
　　Firm-rooted near its highlands.

When war and famine pressed our Isle,
　　Surviving fields of slaughter,
Mountjoy had built his feudal pile
　　By Lua's spreading water. [1]

High towers sentinelled our land,
　　And tiers of bristling cannon
Held seas and harbours in command
　　From Liffy round to Shannon.

Then Coppinger [2] and Roche, [3] as lords,
　　Held fiefs beside Rinn-Mahon :
· For creed and king oft brandished swords
　　That race of Dane and Johan.

Exiled in France or Spain they died,
　　And forfeit all save honour ;
Yet though from Erin parted wide,
　　Their fondest thoughts were on her.

Years passed away with time's advance,
　　Lands, wealth, reward a scion
Of that old lineage, drawn from France,
　　Courageous as the lion.

Blackrock and distant kindred named
　　In grateful recognition,
An aged sire from son had claimed
　　Assent to this petition,

That sailing o'er with golden store,
　　Reward of toil and merit,
True struggling worth near Lua's shore
　　He destined should inherit.

When, previous letters sent by him,
　　Blackrock had reached from Havre,
Young Roche, in vessel tall and trim,
　　Cleft rolling seas that lave her.

That bark flew on with lightning speed,
　　Fresh eastern breezes brought her,
Tow'rds coast-heads known skilled pilots lead,
　　Whilst skimming o'er the water.

Meantime, two kinsmen eager gaze
　　From hills above Dundanion, [4]
Surveying Lee's far winding maze
　　Beyond the deep Lough Mahon.

But as they peer, a swelling gale
  O'er cliff and cape rebounding
Bears to their ears one piercing wail
  Like keener's chant resounding. [5]

A wild shriek rose ! then all was still !
  With fears of threat'ning danger,
His friends descend their lofty hill
  To meet the Gallic stranger.

Out moves a life-yawl from the strand,
  Two stalworth oarsmen rowing
Draw rapid strokes with practised hand,
  Ebb-tide and current flowing.

Full soon, alas ! they heard what fate
  Befell the hapless galley ;
Far under billows sunk its freight
  And crew in wat'ry valley.

On Roche's Point, [6] that ship was driven,
  Wild waves and tempest swelling,
The parting masts, from keelson riven,
  Crash 'midst despair and yelling.

Soon tossed upon the seething deep,
  Pale corpses strew its surges,
Till torn on rugged cliffs they sleep,
  Gulphed down in cavern'd gorges.

One hour before, hopes bright but vain
    Sought friends and cheer the morrow;
That eve sad dirges wake the main
    With plaints of wail and sorrow.

NOTES.

[1] The Castle of Blackrock, to which allusion is here made, erected by Lord Mountjoy in 1604, commands the entrance to Cork city by the river Lee. A pleasing village of the same name lies near the castle, which is built on a limestone promontory, formerly called Rhinn-Mahon. There is a very handsome octagon room within the castle, from which a most delightful view of the river from Cork to Passage may be obtained. The Corporation of Cork formerly held courts of admiralty in this Castle. Having been destroyed by an accidental fire, it was rebuilt in 1829, and was assigned to the mayor of Cork, as an occasional residence, during his official term. Two brilliant lights are displayed from the upper turret. Beautiful villas, mansions and pleasure grounds adorn the immediate neighbourhood.

[2] The Coppingers are of Danish extraction, and have been long settled in the South of Ireland. In the municipal and county affairs of Cork, they have been often entrusted with important offices, and have participated in the disturbances of past periods. In the attainders of 1641 and 1691, some members of this family are found included. Afterwards, many of them rose to distinction in the French and Spanish military service.

[3] At an early period, this family obtained the lordship and territory of Fermoy, in the county of Cork. This district was thenceforward known as the Roche's country. In the city and county of Cork, the Roches always obtained a marked distinction. David de la Roche, the son of Alexander de la Rupe, was the founder of this ancient Norman family in Ireland. He was married to Elizabeth, who was daughter and co-heiress of Gilbert de Clare, Earl of Gloucester, by his wife, King Edward I.'s daughter, the Princess Johan.

Several members of this family became zealous Jacobites, and took up arms for the Stuart cause. As a consequence, they suffered attainder and loss of their estates in 1691. Many retired to the Continent; and several of them entered the Irish Brigades in the service of France.

[4] Dundanion is an elevated position above the castle and village of Blackrock. From this eminence a fine and extended view of the river Lee can be obtained. An Ursuline convent, with a demesne of nearly forty acres, and the remains of some ancient towers are seen at this place.

[5] When a friend or relative dies in a distant part of the country or abroad, a strange wailing voice or sound is heard by members of the family, and in tones of unearthly sadness. The greater may happen to be the space lying between these parties and their lost acquaintance, the louder will such sound be heard. To such a superstition, the Hon. Thomas D'Arcy M'Gee seems to allude in the following beautiful stanza :

> " O Native Land ! dost ever mark
> When the world's din is drowned,
> Betwixt the daylight and the dark
> A wand'ring, solemn sound,
> That on the western wind is borne
> Across thy dewy breast ?
> It is the voice of those who mourn
> For thee, far in the West."

[6] Roche's Point is a rocky promontory at the ocean entrance to Cork Harbour. Some dangerous sunken rocks lie near it, and a light-house, with a coast guard station, has been erected over the jutting headland. The property here belongs to the Roches, and from them the name of this locality has been derived.

No. XVI.

A Legend of Antrim.

SONG OF THE CLURICAUNE.

THE bounding coursers, from their stall,
   Caparisoned for racing speed,
Find riders bold o'er hedge and wall,
   Quite reckless where the hunters lead,
Till panting with their headlong pace
   In circuits round the grassy lawn,
From daring gambols through the chase
   Returns the sporting Cluricaune. [1]

With frolic wild the woods awake,
   Whilst joyous ring our notes of song,
By moonlight o'er the silent lake
   To Antrim's noble pile [2] we throng.
All night within its vaults of wine
   We drain the flowing cups till dawn;
Nor Shane [3] had quaffed in former time
   More freely than the Cluricaune.

NOTES.

[1] By some the Cluricaune is distinguished from the Leprechawn; and the former is said to be of a more jovial disposition than the latter, being fond of good wine and field sports, especially horseracing. He is frequently detected in the act of draining bottles or

drinking generous wine in gentlemen's cellars, and he is usually found astride on a cask or pipe. He is sometimes seen mounted behind a jockey or gentleman rider, on a thorough-bred racer or steeple-chase hunter.

[2] Shane's Castle, the once magnificent residence of Earl O'Neill, was accidently destroyed by fire, in the year 1816. It is delightfully situated on the north-eastern shore of Lough Neagh, about midway on the road leading from Antrim to Randalstown. A charming combination of extensive lake and forest scenery lends every possible interest to this locality. Traces of an older castle and a burial-ground of the once powerful O'Neill family may be found in its immediate neighbourhood. The curiously constructed vaults of this castle lie near the very margin of Antrim bay, which is romantically fringed with woods, around its whole almost semi-circular sweep.

[3] The celebrated and brave chieftain of Clannaboy, Shane O'Neill, was treacherously assassinated by the Scots, in the year 1567. Amongst the alleged defects of his otherwise noble and chivalrous character must be recorded an excessive indulgence in habits of dissipation. It is said—but we may well doubt if on good authority—that his attendants were sometimes obliged to place him chin-deep in an earth-pit, to cool the fevered blood of this intemperate chieftain. Besides the abundant supplies of usquebaugh contained in his cellars, they are reputed to have contained, on ordinary occasions, at least two hundred tuns of the best wine. A visit, which he made to the court of Queen Elizabeth in London, attracted general attention and curiosity, amongst the citizens of that capital. A body-guard of Gallowglasses, armed with battle-axes, and arrayed in the strange costume of their native country, attended this chieftain, in his quality of independent sovereign. By Queen Elizabeth he was received with marked distinction, and for some time after his return to Ireland he displayed apparent zeal in discharging the services required of him.

No. XVII.

A Legend of Lough Gill.

THE BEANSHEE BEETLERS.

By blue Lough Gill [1] at even-tide
The *beanshee* beetlers [2] troop beside
Smooth, stilly waters, circling wide,
    And oft beguile
Their hours of toil with shrill refrain,
Wafting faint echoes o'er the main,
When voices blend in wildest strain
    From Fairy Isle. [3]

NOTES.

[1] The charming scenery of Lough Gill, in the immediate vicinity of Sligo, is justly celebrated. A pleasure boat is easily procurable at the town, and a sail through the channel, conducting to Hazlewood, the enchanting demesne of Mr. Wynne, must afford the most delightful enjoyment. The water, sylvan and mountain scenery will be found combined in duly blended relations to heighten the general effect. This lake is about five miles in length, with a mean average of one mile in breadth, and it is studded with twenty-three islands, nearly all which are adorned with trees. The water-edge acclivities, rising abruptly in some instances whilst sloping gently in others, are often covered with a fine growth of timber. Oak, ash, elm and lime trees flourish in stately luxuriance. The hills around are gracefully posed, and the shore-inlets and promontories lend a great variety of picturesque outline. Some really magnificent views of the lake and

its islands can be obtained by a drive over the roads, which sweep around this fine sheet of water.

[2] Female fairies are often seen beetling linen on the banks of a lonely lake, or near a rocky rivulet, murmuring along the bottom of a winding glen. Whilst beating time with their beetles, they chant wild and plaintive strains, melancholy as the wailing music of an Eolian harp. The songs or music which may be heard near raths obtains the name in Irish of Coel Sᵢᴀ, pronounced *koelshie*, which in English means "fairy-music." It is also said that female fairies are fond of alluring young and handsome huntsmen into their subterranean palaces, and for such purpose they sometimes assume the shape of swift fawns. On this subject, Samuel Lover's much admired song, "The Haunted Spring," has been composed. The following is its opening verse:

> " Gally through the mountain glen
>   The hunter's horn did ring,
>   As the milk-white doe
>   Escaped his bow,
>   Down by the haunted spring.
> In vain his silver horn he wound,
>   'Twas echo answered back;
> For neither groom nor baying hound
>   Were on the hunter's track ;
> In vain he sought the milk-white doe
> That made him stray and 'scaped his bow,
> For, save himself, no living thing
> Was by the silent haunted spring."

[3] The name given to a richly wooded islet of Lough Gill.

No. XVIII.

A Legend of the Glen of Imale.

A CHRISTMAS DAY OF THE PENAL TIMES.

THE sparkling sentinels of night
  Kept vigil through the wintry sky,
The cold moon spread her misty light
  Where hill and vale and cottage lie
Beneath the snow-drift's robe of white.

Young Kieran's head his pillow prest,
  The balm of sleep bedewed his eyes,
With folded arms crossed o'er his breast,
  Whilst measured breathings softly rise
To note the midnight's solemn rest.

Celestial light and visions flew
  In fitful figures through his dreams,
And crowd before his mental view,
  More brightly than the varied hue
That from the rainbow richly streams.

Mov'd by the light of soul that shines
  Through sleep, his comely features glow
And changeful, half-shaped thought defines
  A pleas'd expression o'er his brow,
Which the dark auburn ringlet twines.

Kieran awoke, then clasp'd his hands,
  And kneeling, breathed prayers to Him,
Who rules in Heaven : upraised he stands,
  As if resolving to begin
Some action, which his pray'r demands.

The eve of Christmas-tide had come,
  The morning brought a festal day :
That time no turret's crowning dome
  Rose in our isle, with chiming play
That peal'd for cherished rites of Rome. [1]

Fearing a foe in each lone place,
  Known to a faithful flock, when found,
The outlawed Priest left slightest trace
  Of altar raised on some rude mound,
Or in a ruined chancel's space. [2]

To his poor flock the Bread of Life
  He broke, and taught his followers there,
Though threats of vengeance, words of strife,
  Disturb'd, full oft, the hour of prayer,
And coldly gleamed the murd'rous knife.

But Kieran doubted, where to find
  A glimmer of that distant Thule,
The roof which Priest and altar shrin'd
  For midnight Mass with rites of Yule,
Till Heaven illum'd his wav'ring mind.

He mark'd the mimic scene of sleep,
  And sought the windings of a vale,
Where Christmas vigils peasants keep
  In the lone glen of wild Imale. [3]
Lightly in heart he trod each steep,

Each winding path that led along
  His way, till from a tangled wood
He hears subdu'd the sacred song ;
  And pleased to hear, one moment stood
Before he joined a faithful throng.

Warm shelter from the wintry hoar
  For young and old, that eager press,
A lowly cottage oped its door
  To groups who come and seek ingress,
Whilst snow-tracks damp its earthen floor.

The cheerful flame, with flickering blaze,
  Threw out its ruddy glow and bright,
Around the walls, reflected plays
  Each lambent shade or wave of light
That o'er the rafters dimly strays.

Beneath that thatched and humble shed
  A rustic altar, lightly fram'd,
With linens smoothly overlaid,
  Its mystic range of lights sustain'd,
And ribbon wreaths around were spread.

The Priest was robed in stainless white,
  With flowing alb and tunic wide,
His kneeling flock with streaming eyes
  The opening rites of Mass abide,
Whilst choral stains to Heaven arise.

Young Kieran entered, and askance
  All eyes were bent in doubt and fear,
Mistrustful looks that through each glance,
  Amongst th' assembled swains appear,
Yet mute they gazed, as in a trance.

"Fear not," he cried, " a stranger greets
  His brethren at their Christmas pray'r,
And, blessed be God! whose presence meets
  True worshippers in faith, where'er,
In deserts found, or crowded streets.

"For yestere'en, when kneeling low,
  My mind depress'd with heavy sorrow,
Knew not the place where I might go
  To hear a Mass the coming morrow,
In truth, this heart was filled with woe.

"Yet slumber scarce bedew'd mine eyes,
  When visions hover'd round my bed,
Those very scenes and rites I prize,
  Before my mental view were spread.
With thanks to Heaven, I wake and rise.

"Then, Reverend Father, deign receive
   Th' unworthy son that dares intrude,
Whose grateful transports heartfelt heave,
   To meet you in this solitude,
So dream'd of on the Christmas eve.

"And brethren of the fold, be sure
   No hostile bands my steps attend,
Fear no deceit, nor treacherous lure,
   Believe me well, a faithful friend
Seeks peace and comfort on this floor."

He ceased.   The Priest of God returned,
   "Welcome, my son! be praises given,
The heart that loves is never spurn'd,
   Nor throbs unknown, unpriz'd by Heaven,
In thine, the light of faith hath burn'd.

"As angels sent thee, join thy song
   To swell our humble choral strain,
And kneel thee down, a friend among,
   The faithful few that here remain,
We trust thy looks to do no wrong."

With grateful thanks expressed aloud,
   And deep in soul sincerely felt,
His manly youthful form was bow'd,
   Before the altar, where he knelt,
Most noticed 'midst the peasant crowd.

The morning dawned upon that vale,
   When Mass and sermon had an end,
Departing groups, ere home they steal, [5]
   Give greeting to their stranger friend,
Who westward turned from wild Imale. [6]

Such was the tale to grandson given,
   And treasured long, he tells again
To children gathered round at even,
   Then closing adds, "To mortal ken
Mysterious are the ways of Heaven!"

NOTES.

[1] In reference to the disastrous results of penal legislation in these realms, an Irish writer, Aubrey de Vere, alludes to

   "the sons of Ireland, far and near,
   Amerced of altar priest and sacrifice."

The silence of the grave would have settled completely over that state of indignant feeling and covert disaffection, which pervaded the minds of Irish Catholics, during the earlier part of the last century, had we no other medium for forming an estimate of their intensity and vitality, than the printed records and published literature of Ireland and Great Britain. In my school-boy days, I have heard the present legend or narrative related by an intelligent, enthusiastically patriotic and religious young artizan, as having been communicated to himself, by a trustworthy and venerated grandfather. If I have selected my own mode of treatment and disregarded the *ipsissima verba* of a simple and affecting incidental romantic statement of the penal days, I have presented substantially the plot, place and circumstances, connected with this curious tradition. The period, to which it refers, must be assigned to the earlier portion of the eighteenth century.   4

[2] I recollect having pointed out to me the exact places, in three different instances, where a priest formerly met his congregation to offer up the Holy Sacrifice of Mass in the open air. One of these places bears the name " Chapel Hill," to the present day. The other spot selected for religious exercises was in the midst of a dense wood of primeval growth. The third station was under the side of a rocky hill, which presented a sheltered and secluded situation, yet only during fair weather : its commanding position also afforded opportunity for friendly scouts to give warning of any approaching danger. These three localities are to be seen in the eastern province of Ireland. In the western province, at the present advanced period of civilization and tolerance, I have stood on two different sites, where the people assembled on Sundays and holidays of obligation, without a roof to cover their heads, during the heats of summer or the cold blasts of winter. One of these sites, in the county of Mayo, lies within the walls of the fine old abbey of Ballintubber, so romantically situated with a surrounding of varied scenery, but sadly disfigured by a Vandalic attempt at restoration. Before the blighting years of famine in 1847 and 1848, an effort had been made to roof the building for purposes of Catholic worship; but hunger, emigration and pestilence covered the fair face of this enchanting region, nor have the energies of pastor or people been able since to effect an object so essential and desirable. The other instance to which I allude was furnished within a prosperous town in the county of Galway, where the landed proprietor refused a site for church building to his own tenants. The whole Catholic population was obliged to kneel down in a public market place, adjoining the main street, and exposed *sub Dio* to the varying inclemency of the seasons. It must be long, indeed, before all the traces of our penal code and the evils of a vicious social system will totally disappear from our misgoverned Island. The following passage, from a legendary and historical poem of Aubrey de Vere, although bearing allusion to a different subject, will apply with peculiar force to the present versified tradition :

> " O ! when will it leave me, that widows' wail ?
> My heart is stone and my brain is fire
> For the men that died in thy woods, Imayle !"

[3] The romantic glen of Imale stretches along the head waters of the river Slaney, which descend from the sides of the towering Lugnaquilla and Table mountains. The several branching and precipitously running streams unite in this enchanting vale and flow westward through the parish of Donoughmore, in the barony of Upper Talbotstown and county of Wicklow. Wild and rugged features contrast with the softer and more agreeable aspects of nature in this lonely region. Fertile tracts of pasturage skirt the picturesque and winding course of the river, whilst pretty mansions and plantations occasionally diversify its prospects. According to a note in the *Feilire Aenghuis* and in O'Clerigh's Irish Calendar at the 7th of October, Glendalough is said to be situated within the territory of Ui Mail (Imale). In this district, the O'Tooles settled, after their expulsion from Ui Muireadhaigh, in the present county of Kildare. In an old life of St. Kevin, quoted by Ussher and by the Bollandists, it is said that the church of *Gleann Da Loch*, i. e. *Vallis duorum stagnorum*, lay within the territory *Forthuatha*, or *the stranger tribe*. Hence it would appear, that Forthuatha and Ui Mail were formerly convertible appellations for the same district of country.

[4] Towards the close of William III.'s reign, various articles of the Treaty of Limerick were shamefully violated, by an imposition of severe restrictions on the Catholics of Ireland. An act of the Irish Parliament, intended " to prevent the further growth of Popery," was passed into a law, during the second year of Queen Anne's reign, A. D. 1703. By a subsequent statute, if an unregistered priest were detected, a heavy fine was imposed on the Papists—as they were insultingly termed—of the county, where he was discovered, and the proceeds were directed to be paid as a reward for the informer. This provision soon created a miscreant class of detectives, usually denominated " priest-hunters," who obtained fifty pounds per head for the discovery of an archbishop, a bishop or an ecclesiastical superior, and twenty pounds were given for the prosecution of other ecclesiastics. In the old grave-yard of Ballintobber, county of Mayo, I stood beside the grave of *Shawn na Soygarth*, whose infamous proceedings in this line have been preserved amongst local popular traditions, and have formed the subject of an interesting novel, by Mr. Archdekin. The most singular

feature is here presented in a bended tree, that like the Indian banyan
turns down its branches, which take root in the earth and spread over
the grave, because, as the people believe, its trunk could not tend
upwards to Heaven, in such a close proximity with the execrated remains of the "priest-catcher." A Portuguese Jew, named Garcia,
living in Dublin, assumed various disguises, and sometimes appeared
in the outward garb of a priest, that he might obtain from unsuspecting
Catholics information regarding the haunts of their clergy. In 1718,
he succeeded in arresting seven unregistered priests, who were banished the kingdom. The usual punishment, inflicted on the arrested
ecclesiastics, was incarceration and transportation beyond the seas: in
case of their returning to Ireland, they were adjudged to have been
guilty of treason, and the legal penalty was an ignominious death.
In several instances, the gentry and magistrates, through prejudiced
and bigoted motives or through a misguided opinion of official duty,
joined in the pursuit of priests. I have been shown the exact spot,
where a lord of the manor is said to have taken his station with
some of his myrmidons to arrest a clergyman in the penal days.
This intention was however defeated by information of the plot,
which had been communicated to the priest. During this state of
affairs, numbers of the regular clergy and unregistered seculars became exiles or on being apprehended were cast into prison and afterwards transported. The pious and learned De Burgo, Bishop of
Ossory, who was a contemporary with many of his persecuted order,
tells us, that only a few clergymen remained in the kingdom, who
were not able to leave on account of old age or infirmity. These took
refuge in caves and other hiding places. To the credit of many bene-
volent Protestants, it must be recorded, that they offered shelter and
hospitality to officiating priests in their own houses, which would be
most likely to remove all suspicion of concealing the proscribed. In
many instances, the priest-hunter's occupation became so exceedingly
odious both to Protestants and Catholics, that ruffians pursuing this
detestable calling were assailed with clubs and showers of stones, flung
at them when appearing in public, by members of both denominations. However, Parliament had decreed, "that the prosecuting and
informing against Papists was an honourable service, and that all

magistrates who neglected to execute these laws were betrayers of the liberties of the kingdom." It is scarcely to be doubted, that many were found willing to " better the instruction," when this vile occupation of priest-catching was thus sought to be rendered respectable by legal enactment, although social usages, charitable commiseration and correct feeling might have greatly moderated the effects of such intolerant and cruel legislation.

[5] The long civic and religious persecution, impoliticly inflicted on Irish Catholics, during the last century, left them, as a community, thoroughly disaffected to the existing government of that period. Regarding such a state of feeling, the allegorical and Jacobite ballads which remain furnish incontestible evidences. It is also interesting and instructive to compare Irish Jacobite songs of the last century, differing materially in tone and sentiment, with the " Jacobite Relics of Scotland," which have been so carefully collected and illustrated by James Hogg, "the Ettrick Shepherd." Whilst these latter effusions breathe defiance, bitter sarcasm, pointed satire, undisguised seditious personalities, contemptuous allusion and energetic denunciation of the Hanoverian line, as sung at social parties and gatherings ; the former compositions are usually desponding, timidly veiled under allegory, only fully divined by the initiated, and specially destined for covert vocalism or confidential circulation, amongst avowed adherents of the Stuart family. I have heard a curious tradition, yet current in the southern part of Kilkenny county, illustrating the anxiety felt to welcome Prince Charles Edward Stuart to Ireland. The Rev. James Comerford, P.P. of Innistiogue, had fought as a soldier in the Irish Brigade at Fontenoy, and after his return to Ireland, having embraced the clerical state, he did not cease to keep up a constant correspondence with friends on the Continent, regarding the project of a French invasion of Ireland. Having satisfied himself, that the Prince, with his Irish and French retinue, would land at or near Waterford, this priest is said to have felt such a nervous anxiety about the issue, that he was known frequently during each day to put his ear close to the ground, in order to ascertain, whether the French war-ships and cannon were opening fire on the Fort of Duncannon. He was also constantly engaged making inquiries of all coming from that quarter, if they had

heard any news about the Prince's arrival. This priest, whose name occurs amongst the subscribers to De Burgo's *Hibernia Dominicana*, had made all preparations to rise in arms, with his parishioners, when the young Pretender should have landed on our shores, as had been expected and most earnestly desired. Amongst the *Ballads of Ireland*, collected and edited by Edward Hayes, there is one. by some anonymous writer, which admirably details the effects of penal legislation. Thus run its opening lines:

" In that dark time of cruel wrong, when on our country's breast
  A dreary load, a ruthless code, with wasting terrors prest—
  Our gentry, stript of land and clan, sent exiles o'er the main,
  To turn the scales on foreign fields for foreign monarchs' gain—
  Our people trod like vermin down, all fenceless flung to sate
  Extortion, lust, and brutal whim, and rancorous bigot hate—
  Our priesthood tracked from cave to hut, like felons chased and lashed,
  And from their ministering hands the lifted chalice dashed ;
  In that black time of law-wrought crime, of stifling woe and thrall,
  There stood supreme one foul device, one engine worse than all ;
  Him whom they wished to keep a slave, they sought to make a brute—
  They banned the light of heaven—they bade instruction's voice be mute."

[6] The distance, which this humble peasant had been obliged to travel in order to assist at the Holy Sacrifice of Mass, must have exceeded twenty miles. There are some MS. Letters of the Venerable Charles O'Conor of Balenagar yet extant, in our public libraries, which present in confidential and private correspondence the religious privations to which Catholics in his province had been subjected, during these dark days of intolerance and persecution.

No. XIX.

A Legend of the Coast of Clare.

TIR NA N-OG.

Out through the misty waves,
    Far from Liscannor, [1]
Lie in their hidden caves
    Plains of a manor,
Arched o'er with crystal tide,
    Fretful in motion,
And spacious as desert wide,
    Spread under ocean.

Fair are those elfin haunts
    Set round with flowers;
Nor Tir na n-og's realm [2] wants
    Thick leafy bowers;
Amber hues brightly gleam
    Over pure fountains;
Clear flows each silver stream
    Gushing from mountains.

Smooth are the spreading lakes,
    Cooped in their valleys;
Purple the light that breaks,
    Through glades and alleys.

On pastures are heard and seen
   Milk-white herds lowing,
Vine-stalks are waving green,
   Their luscious fruits growing.

Wild thyme and fern shade
   Herb-covered ledges,
Red roses twining braid
   Jasmine-copsed hedges :
Tall castles are rising fair,
   The rich lawns adorning,
These scented as mountain air
   With breath of the morning.

Immortals, in youthful bands, [8]
   Joyous inherit
Th' unfading and beauteous lands
   Of parted spirit ;
Niamh, through Kill Stuifin gate
   Nether depths wading,
Points to their blissful state,
   Sons of men leading. [4]

Friends, that remain on earth,
   May pine broken-hearted,   ·
When rise to a newer birth
   Loved ones departed.
These plac'd in lasting home,
   O'er their bridge speeding, [5]
Peaceful for ever roam,
   Time's flight unheeding.

NOTES.

[1] The Irish stories of Cᵼη ηⱥ η-óʒ, *Thir-na-nog*, or the Land of Youth, are highly imaginative. This charming region of the Immor-tals is so called, because those who dwell there are not affected by any changes of time, and because they live in a state of perpetual youth-fulness. The territory abounds in all manner of delights, and it lies deeply buried, as some suppose, under the waters of the larger lakes of Ireland. But a position more universally assigned to it, is near the farthest bound of a misty horizon, on the Atlantic Ocean. We are told, that there are different entrances or passages to it from various parts of the western shores of our Island. In Liscannor Bay, on the western coast of Clare county, there is a spot indicated, between Lis-cannor and Lahinch, called Cᵼll Sᴄuᵼꜰꞎη, Kill Stuifin, which is always marked with white breaking waves. These are supposed to have been caused by the shallowness of water, rolling over a submerged and an enchanted city. By some, this city is seen once in seven years; but those who observe it are sure to disappear from this life, before the close of that ensuing septeniad. They do not die, however, but transmigrate to the Land of Youth, where they remain in a per-petual state of bloom, vigor, health and happiness. Those favoured with sight of the sub-marine city are supposed to be endowed with a prophetic spirit, until removed from this world. Previous to their entrance within the bowers of their distant elysium, mortals pass under the waves, through that magic passage shown to them during life.

[2] Amongst the Irish national legends, published by the Ossianic Society, there will be found an interesting account of Tir na n-og, as related by the ancient bard Oisin to St. Patrick. This tract is trans-ated and edited by Mr. Bryan O'Looney. Subsequent to the battle of Gabhra, or Garristown, fought on the 17th of June, A. D. 283, when Oscar was slain, after Finn and his heroes had been fatigued with hunting, on the shores of Loch Lein, a beautiful maiden, riding on a steed, approached them. On being accosted, she announced herself as Niamh, daughter of the king of Youth. She declared her love for

Finn's son Oisin, and gave such a glowing picture of the invisible realms where she dwelt, that the bard was induced to accompany his *inamorata*, mounted behind her on a steed, to "the mouth of the great sea." Here parting from Finn, we have a wonderful account of their journey through the waves, whilst his female guide explains to her lover all the wonders, which he now beheld for the first time. After a prolonged contest, when Oisin had conquered Fomhor Builleach, *the striking giant*, of Dromloghach, and had delivered a queen confined in his fortress, this adventurous bard enters the enchanted land, which is most romantically described. Here, with consent of its king and queen, he espoused the "golden-headed Niamh," and this immortal bride bore him two sons and a daughter. These children were respectively placed as rulers over Ꞇꞁꞃ ꞁꜳ ꞁ-óꞡ, the Land of Youth, Ꞇꞁꞃ ꞁꜳ ꞃ-beo, the Land of the Living, and Ꞇꞁꞃ ꞁꜳ ꞃ-buꜳꞁꜳ, the Land of Virtues. These are supposed to have been the three districts, into which the ocean kingdom of happiness had been divided. Ossian called his preternatural sons, one after his natural father Fionn, and the other after his terrestrial son, Oscar, whilst to the daughter he gave the name Plur-na-mban, *the flower of women*. After a long delay in the Land of Youth, Ossian, taking leave of his wife and children for ever, returned to Ireland, where he finds that Fionn and his Fianna heroes had long before departed from green Erin, whilst their halls of Almhuin in Leinster were left completely deserted and overgrown with nettles and weeds.

[3] Besides all the delights that can be conceived, as abounding in the Land of Youth, those who enter it, usually in the bloom of life, never afterwards become either older or younger in appearance. The Land of the Living was thought to give perpetual life to departed spirits of the just, and it is said to lie near the sun's setting. This territory is approachable through the seas, lakes, rivers, raths, duns and forts of Ireland. The Land of Virtues, indicated by its title, confers on its inhabitants those enjoyments, which are the best reward of a well spent life. Sometimes it is called the Land of Victories, probably in allusion to great felicity, consequent on a successful cessation of earthly conflicts. These remarkable opinions are supposed to have been entertained by the early Milesian colonists of this island, and are

curious, as illustrating their speculations regarding futurity. Amongst the Danes, also, a supposition yet lingers, that a buried city lies under the ocean waves, around their shores; and sometimes they imagine a faint, sweet music, together with a chime of church bells, may be heard wafted across the billows to the ears of a lonely wanderer on the beach.

[4] Near Lahinch, there is an elevation called, Cnoc na Sío-guiòe, or Fairy Hill, where, it is said, the nobles of Tir na n-og hold conferences with the fairy gentles there living. These latter are presumed to be the spies or agents of Immortals beyond the waves, and they always report, when a young and beautiful subject for this Land of Youth may be found in the adjoining neighbourhood. Then the golden-haired Niamh makes her appearance to the young man or woman, destined for abduction, and she afterwards vanishes from sight. Soon after will the visited person pine away, and appear dead to all friends and acquaintances; but in reality, it is fabled, that the future abode of such person is in the shadowy land of perpetual youth.

[5] The pagan Irish imagined the just would pass into a Paradise, consisting of two Islands. One of these, the Land of the Young, was supposed to confer a happiness superior to the other, known as the Land of the Living. Before entering into either Elysium, however, such spirits were obliged to pass over bpoiceaḃ a n-aen pibe, *the bridge of one hair*. This imaginary structure spread out sufficiently wide to afford a safe passage for the just. It contracted to the breadth of a single hair, for the wicked, who fell from it, to assume different shapes of animals in this world, as a species of preparation, before they would be qualified to pass in safety over the mysterious bridge.

No. XX.

A Legend of Sliebe Donard.

THE GANCONERS.

Slieve Donard looms high o'er the mountains of Mourne, [1]
Down its bleak, shelving sides rushing torrents have worn
Yawning chasms through granite, disruptured and torn.

From the grey cairn o'ertopping, deserted and bare,
Captain Dearg [2] and his *ganconers*, [3] riding through air,
Whilst early dawn blushes, spring up from that lair.

And they sweep over hills, plains or valleys of Erin,
When hosts of Finn Varrah [4] are met on Slieve Guil-
  lin, [5]
In the caves of Keis-Corainn, [6] on lofty Knockferin. [7]

By the side of lone Croghan [8] the milk-maid sings blithely
Till the *ganconer* horsemen whisk onward so sprightly,
Their armour and swords in the sun sparkling brightly.

An opening beneath the fern-thicket is seen,
Where Dearg's fairy host hides its panoplied sheen,
Far down in the depths of that hill-side so green.

Then soon from the summit of Croghan arise
Whole legions of cavaliers dazzling the eyes,
With myriad gay pennons afloat in the skies.

What bodes such a portent few mortals can dream!
Why ride they in force, while their flashing swords gleam,
Or speed with the swiftness of passing sunbeam?

They must travel ere nightfall, those famed fairy men,
And troop midst the wild-wood, waste moorland or fen,
Many raths shall they visit, through dingle and glen.

When dusky Slieve Donard is veiled from the sight,
Captain Dearg leads his *ganconers* home for the night,
And they rest in grand halls till the first dawn of light.

Yet when a loud clarion-note rings from the horn,
While the soldier-bands rustle through blades of green corn,
Purple *lusmores* [9] bend lowly and dew-gemm'd at morn.

NOTES.

[1] Some of the wildest and most sublime scenery in Ireland may be found amongst the Mourne Mountains, which rise majestically over the eastern shores of Down county, between the bay of Carlingford and that of Dundrum. Slieve Donard dominates far above the other steeps of this range, at a height of 2,796 feet over the sea. The prospect from this elevated cone, on a clear day, is vast beyond conception; and several small streams take their course from it in every direction. Although granite is the prevailing geologic formation; yet a great variety of different constituents may be traced throughout this mountainous district. Mineral productions also abound. The Mourne mountains for the most part lie within a barony bearing the same name. There is a curious local tradition given by the late Dr. O'Donovan, in his MS. Ordnance Survey antiquarian letter, relating to the county of Down. There it is said, that Slieve Donard derived its name from an ancient chieftain called Donnart, who was miraculously converted by St. Patrick, and who abandoned his former fortified resi-

dence, with the sports of hunting, to betake himself to a life of prayer and fasting, on the apex of this wild mountain of Donard. All these particulars are not presented, however, in the Life of St. Domangard, as published by Colgan in the *Acta Sanctorum Hiberniæ*, at the 24th day of March. Local residents show the altar of St. Donnaght (as Domangard is now called) at the north-western cairn of Slieve Donard. Here it is thought the saint yet appears to celebrate mass every Sunday. If report speak true, there is a cave, running from the sea-shore at the south of Newcastle to the very summit of Slieve Donard. Through this cavity some men are said to have ventured to the summit of this mountain, until they were met by the patron saint in his robes. He warned them not to prosecute their adventure farther. Amongst the Ordnance Survey Letters on the county of Down, at present preserved in the Royal Irish Academy, the late Dr. O'Donovan, in a letter, dated Castlewellan, April 23rd, 1834, pp. 92 to 94, gives; us the following interesting account of his ascending Slieve Donard : " I have this day made a pilgrimage to the summit of Sliabh Domhanghairt. I have been induced to perform this pilgrimage from many motives. 1. To endeavour to get the names of the Mourne mountains from its lofty summit, and for this purpose I have employed a guide, but in this, I have been much disappointed. Of this, however, I shall speak hereafter. 2. To gratify a curiosity excited in my mind, by the gigantic appearance of the mountain itself, from every part of the county, and by the following passage in Colgan's *Acta SS.*: ' In the territory of Iveagh and diocese of Dromore there are two churches dedicated to St. Domangard, one (which is at the foot of a very high mountain overhanging the eastern sea) is called *Rath Murbhuilg* by the ancients, but at this day *Machaire Ratha ;* the other on the summit of that lofty mountain, far removed from the habitation of every human being, and which is frequented by great multitudes of pilgrims, &c. Hence this mountain, which was called Sliabh Slainge by the ancients, is at this day commonly called Sliabh Domhangaird from this saint.' . . . . When at Newcastle, I had imagined that I could run up the top of it in a few minutes ; but I soon learned I had to climb a mountainous region, never since the creation subdued by the hand of cultivation, and never destined to alter its primeval features, until the world shall be resolved into its ultimate elements. The ascent from Newcastle is difficult and dangerous, in consequence of the rocky and steep surface of the passage, which leads to the base of Slieve Donard. In this passage, you are guided for the distance of a mile by a mountain stream, now almost dried up, but in winter precipitous and large, as its wide and well washed rocky channel sufficiently shows. This stream is said to divide the Millstone Mountain from Thomas Mountain—two very high mountains situated at the base of Slieve Donard to the N.E. and N., and originally considered a part of it, before these mountains received separate names. When you arrive at the source of this stream, you turn towards the west, a little above the summit of Thomas Mountain, where the ground, though rugged and full of holes, becomes comparatively level. This is called the *top of the hill* by the country people, who do not include it in the Millstone Mountain, Thomas Mountain or Slieve Donard. From this place, Donard is seen towering majestically and awfully above the neighbouring mountains, which, though they present a grand appearance from Newcastle, here sink into comparative insignificance—not because they are so much lower than Donard, but because that mountain is magnified and rendered stupendous by its overhanging contiguity, and the others are diminished by distance and comparison. Up this steep and rocky passage I skipped from stone to stone, with great agility, but was obliged to wait for my guide, whom age had rendered less vigorous. I gained the top, and looked around in every direction, astonished and amazed,

'Till contemplation had her fill.'

As the prospect from the summit of this mountain is so well known, and as you yourself have been on it, I shall avoid foolish descriptions; but I cannot avoid writing down a few thoughts, that struck my mind very forcibly. There are two circular *cairns* on its summit, one to the N.E., and the other to the S.W.: the former is now much destroyed, and the well, which my guide informs me was *springing* in the centre of it, filled up with stones. This he says was done by the *sappers*. If it were they who filled this well with stones, they seem to have had very little to do! But my opinion is, that it was done by some *devout* visitor, who thought it his duty to destroy every vestige of superstition. The *cairn* to the S.W. is much more perfect, but destroyed in a great measure to erect the Trigonometrical station, which in the course of ages may puzzle antiquarians to discover its scientific use. The well in this cairn is now dried up, and I can scarcely believe that it ever contained spring water. To the east of the well there is a stone, which to me appears to have been used by the saint as an altar, and it would also appear probable, that he had roofed this *cairn*, and used it as a little ' chapple.' This conjecture is corroborated by the fact that Sir William Petty called it a ' chapple,' and Colgan ' a church.' I am also of opinion, that this *cairn* had been originally used as a druidical place of worship, and that the hermit took advantage of the pile, as the sappers have of the ' chapple,' to form a little house and place of worship for himself and his visitors. I cannot dismiss this subject, without remarking what great enthusiasm and love of retirement must have induced any human being to fix his residence here ' far from the abodes of men,' on the highest peak of a wild and dismal region of the most barren mountains, exposed to every storm, and far removed from every land producing food for the sustinence of man! For to this day, there is not a human being to be seen throughout the mountains and valleys, for a considerable extent in any direction! The region is dismal, lonely and desolate, and will remain so to the end of time; its rocky and ruggedly steep surface defying the hand of cultivation. Notwithstanding all this, I am fully convinced that St. Donard lived for some time on the summit of Slieve Slainge, to which he left his name; because the fame of a holy man who cured the sick, and restored sight to the blind, would soon draw to his cell a number of visitors, who never failed to offer him gifts, and supply him daily, perhaps hourly, with food. I am of opinion that Donard had lived here as a hermit, before he established his *nobile monasterium*, and his lofty *claig-theach*, at the foot of his mountain. And here let me remark, by way of digression, that all the young people who *have read* call this a Round Tower of unknown use; but all the old people who have never read any book but their prayer books, and who do not understand the meaning of *Round Towers*, call it the *claigtheach*, and tell you with a positiveness, not to be contradicted, that it was the *belfry* belonging to the old church. From the summit of Slieve Donard, the parish of Magheraw appears as level as the surface of the ocean. I was forcibly struck with the applicability of the name, as I looked down upon it, from the 'chapple' of St. Donard, and I was also struck with the aptness of its ancient name of *Rath Murbulg* or the *fort of the belly of the sea*. The process, by which the human mind arrives at truth in any train of inquiry, is curious, and worthy of our attention. While sitting on the *apex* of Slieve Donard, I made a very important discovery in our ancient topography, and cleared up to my own satisfaction, what I was a long time puzzled about, viz., the situation of Rath Murbhulg in Dalaradia, and that of Murbholg Dal Riada. Both retain the name to this day. Murbholg in Dalaradia is Murlough bay in the County of Down, between Newcastle and Dundrum, and Murbholg Dalriada is Murlogh in the County of Antrim." To this letter Mr. O'Donovan adds the following interesting postscript : "The Sappers have left a good many circular cairns on this mountain. I hope these will never be taken for Druids circles or 'chapples' of hermits, though I am fully convinced, that their sojourn on this mountain will be handed down to posterity. I must leave the two parishes of Mourne for the last, as I cannot possibly ascertain all the names of mountains, streams, loughs, rocks, &c. in them, without either a map, giving all the names that are to be engraved, or a perfect list of all such names, accompanied by accurate descriptions of their situations and features, so as to prevent me from mistaking any one name for another like it. I have found from experience, that either is absolutely necessary; the latter would be less trouble to me, but both would ensure more certainty. You will immediately perceive the necessity of this, when you consider how difficult it is, for any one, or two, or four, to remember all the streams, rocks, hills, &c. in any one parish, and how easily some of their names might be omitted without some help. Those who have surveyed the land, who have lived in the neighbourhood, and who have with their own eyes seen these features, should furnish a list of their names, spelled as well as they could catch the sound. If this be done, I can ascertain the correct name without much trouble, by consulting one, two or three intelligent

persons in every parish ; but if I were to traverse every townland, to
see every stream and rock in it that bears a name, it would take me a
life-time to go through one county.—*Tuesday night*, 11 *o'Clock*."
(Ibid. p. 95.) The map to which allusion is made, as being in contemplation, it appears was afterwards executed by Mr. O'Donovan, and it
is to be found, at present, appended to his Down Letters. It embraces
the parish of Kilkeel, which is the only one in, and commensurate in
extent with, the Barony of Mourne. On this map are accurately and
beautifully marked the ancient and modern names of places—the former in Irish characters. Some of these names are only written in
pencil marks. It would be desirable, they were more permanently
noted in ink, before they become altogether illegible. With regard to
the name of Kilkeel parish, he observes on the opposite page, " Cıll ᴀ'
Ċᴀoıl, i. e. the Church of *Caol*, the founder, who was so called, according to tradition, from the *slender* form of his body."

[2] Captain Dearg, or the Red Captain, is the chief amongst a
tribe of Ulster fairies, and he is often seen riding through the air
with his merrymen.

[3] In the North of Ireland the fairies are called *ganconers*, and
" wee people."

[4] Finn Varrah and his fairy host live in the subterranean halls
of the hill of Knockmaah, in the County of Galway. They often visit
distant places, which are considered the favourite haunts of the airy
sprites in Connaught and Ulster. Setting out from smooth Knockmaah, they ride on fleet coursers, from the dawn of day to night-fall.
The following itinerant chase, and to very distant places, is quoted
from Dr. Neilson's Irish Grammar, in T. Crofton Croker's *Researches
in the South of Ireland*, chap. v. :

> " Around Knock Greine and Knock-na-Rae,
> Ben Bulbin and Keis-Corainn,
> To Ben Echlaon and Loch Da éan,
> Thence north-east to Sliabh Gullin.
> They travelled the lofty hills of Mourne,
> Round high Sliabh Donard and Ballachanèry,
> Down to Dundrinn, Dundrum and Dunardsey,
> Right forward to Knock-na-Feadala."

[5] Slieve Guillion, a mountain, dividing in part the parishes of

Killevy and Forkill, is situated in the barony of Upper Orior, county of Armagh. It rises 1,893 feet over the sea-level, and overlooks a beautiful district of country. On the top of this mountain, a large cairn or sepulchral monument may be seen. It is supposed to have been the tomb of Cualgne, son of Breogan, one of the Milesian chieftains. He fell in battle on the plain beneath, and it is supposed, that from him has been derived the name of this mountain, and the adjoining district. Killevy Lodge and Hawthorn Hill—two beautiful demesnes—are seen on the eastern slopes. Camlough lake and mountain also lie near Slieve Guillion. This locality is celebrated in a poem, ascribed to the bard Ossian, and called in Irish, *Laoi na Sealga*, elegantly translated by Miss Brooke, in "the Chace."

[6] The Caves of Keis-Corainn, in a mountain bearing a like name, are situated in the barony of Corran, county of Sligo. For an illustration of these remarkable caves and curious legends, quoted from the topographical tract, called the Duinseanchus, the reader is referred to Dr. Petrie's account, contained in the *Irish Penny Journal*, vol. I. p. 9. A gentle and skilful harper, or ollave, named Corann, is said to have received this territory free from the Tuatha de Danann, as a reward for his musical and astrological accomplishments.

[7] Knockferin (otherwise Knockfierna) is a high hill near Ballingarry, county of Limerick. On its top, a conical pile has been raised, and this is said to have been the site of an ancient temple. This place is sometimes called by the Irish bards, Cnoc Dónn Ḟiṁiṁeaċ. It is supposed to have derived its name from Donn, king of the Munster Fairies. It is also mentioned amongst the following haunted places, famed in fairy topography, and which are introduced in Edward Walsh's Munster Keen of a bereaved wife, lamenting her deceased husband:

> "I still might hope, did I not thus behold thee,'
> That high Knockferin's airy peak might hold thee,
> Or Crohan's fairy halls, or Corrin's towers,
> Or Lene's bright caves, or Cleana's magic bowers."

[8] Croghan hill is a remarkable eminence in the barony of Lower Philipstown in the King's county and on the borders of Westmeath. Several holy wells and objects of antiquity are seen in its immediate

vicinage. An unenclosed grave-yard, with its head-stones, lies on the eastern slope. The grand panoramic view from its summit extends in an unintercepted line over a level country and to an immense distance. According to the common opinion, this hill is considered a head-quarters or mustering-ground for all the Irish fairies. It is comme-morated in Spencer's "Faerie Queen." There is another celebrated spot called Rath-Croghan, which is situated in the parish of Elphin and County of Roscommon. This is remarkable for an ancient burial ground and several curious caves in its neighbourhood. It is said to have been a site chosen for inaugurating the ancient kings of Con-naught. Different moats are seen near the cross-roads at Rath-Croghan. Here the fairies are said always to have assembled in great numbers.

[9] The bells of a beautiful plant, designated in Irish, lus-mọn, Anglicised "the great herb," known to botanists as the *Digitalis Pur-purea*, and called "Fairy cap," or "Fairies' thimble," by the common people, is so named, from its fancied resemblance to their crowning coifs. It is supposed, that this plant bends its long stalks, as a token of recognition and salute to passing supernatural beings. In summer's sunshine, fairies often sleep in the pendant purple bells of the beauti-ful plant, known as the wild *Campanula*. It is called Fox-glove, which is supposed by some to be a corruption of "Folks'" or "good Folks' glove." Artists are fond of depicting the elfin tribe wearing coronets of such flowers.

No. XXI.

A Legend of Killarney.

THE SILVER OAR.

A SILVER oar its watery grave
Finds low beneath Killarney's wave,
And Bran, the dog of Ossian's chase,
Guards well that deep, enchanted place. [1]

Nor would the boldest diver there
A contest with this guardian dare,
Whose steady orbs their vigils keep
O'er that prized treasure of the deep.

Yet Bran shall close his wakeful eyes:
Then, he who first attempts the prize
Shall bear it from these depths away,
Above the wave to light and day. [2]

NOTES.

[1] The celebrated wolf-hound of Fingal and Ossian is found in connexion with many an Irish legend. Although Bran is said to rest under the waves of Killarney, until his enchantment be broken in the manner above related; yet, according to another statement, he is said to have taken a last leap from a cliff, called Creggy-Bran, over the small lake Ziernach Bran, in the county of Clare. Fingal, whilst engaged in hunting on the mountains of Callaw, started a snow-white

hart, with hoofs of gold, which, after a long course, jumped from the cliff already named, followed by Bran. Both hart and dog plunged beneath the surface of that lake and again rose—the former in the shape of a beautiful lady, who, laying her hand on the head of Bran, consigned him for ever to the depths of a lake, which the peasantry believe to be fathomless.

[2] The boatmen of Killarney relate many other stories, regarding the subaqueous wonders of their world-renowned lakes. Thus, there are certain rocky caves, near the shores, and which seem to extend under the surface water of the lough, which are called the Earl of Desmond's " wine vaults," and where, it is said, this mystic personage guards his vinous stores. Indeed, the genuineness of many legends, related by the boatmen, may well be questioned; for one of them very candidly acknowledged to the writer, that his class commonly studied the tastes and dispositions of different tourists, and if the latter felt inclined to hear of marvellous incidents, legends in abundance could be fabricated, for the entertainment of such patrons. With visitors more seriously disposed, the guides are less communicative; but without some indulgence in their usual exaggerated narratives, a day on the lakes loses much of its interest and attraction.

No. XXII.

A Legend of Clonenagh.

SAINT FINTAN'S ROAD.

THE night-clouds were dark, holy Fintan [1] returning,
    Dun, dreary and dismal the prospect before,
      As feebly he journeyed, foot-sore ;
No bright lunar orb in the starless sky burning,
    Soft yielding each step that morass scarce bore,
      For quagmires had sprinkled it o'er.

" Dear grey abbey-walls," said the saint while approaching,
    " Oh, when shall I find your delightful repose,
      On the fertile and grass-bearing knowes :
The tempest howls over on wild moss encroaching,
    Tall pines of the wilderness bend as it blows,
      And the danger more fearfully grows !"

Pious peasants relate, how that tempest then ceasing
    Unveiled the bright moon, from a covert of shade,
      In all her true glories arrayed,
When a clear shining star, through the liquid air chasing,
    Led on to his churches [2] a road newly made,
      And in calm were the soughing winds laid.

Even yet, at the lone hour of midnight returning,
    Swains tread on with joy, o'er that causeway secure,
      For their patron will safety insure ;

Nor fear they if midnight be shadowed in mourning,
　Whilst telling their prayers, devoutly and pure,
　　To Fintan, the saint of that moor. [8]

NOTES.

[1] The old Acts of St. Fintan, Abbot of Clonenagh, are published by Colgan, in the *Acta Sanctorum Hiberniæ*, at the 17th of February. On this day, his festival is yet devoutly celebrated in the parish.
A new and beautiful Catholic Church has been recently erected, under
this saint's invocation, in the adjoining town of Mountrath, according
to designs furnished by an eminent architect, John S. Butler, Esq., of
Dublin. St. Fintan flourished early in the sixth century.

[2] Peasants living in the neighbourhood of Clonenagh yet under-
take to point out the site of its Seven Churches, which they say had a
former existence, and were situated on as many indicated green mounds,
according to tradition. The fertile and elevated *oasis*, on which the
ruins and grave-yards of Clonenagh may be observed, at the present
day, is almost completely insulated by an extensive tract of bog. The
old ruins yet remaining had been roofed and used as the Protestant
Church of Clonenagh parish, probably within the memory of persons
yet living. Evidences of this fact yet remain, in the shape of plais-
tered walls and rather modern additions to the old masonry. The surrounding grave-yard, shaded with venerable ash-trees, is the favourite
burial place of Protestants; although, as may be supposed, the number of Catholics interred even here considerably preponderates. On
the opposite side of a road, leading from Maryborough to Mountrath, there is another grave-yard, which is used exclusively as the
burial-ground of Catholics. This latter contains a great number of
graves, and rises to a considerable elevation, above the road-level and
adjoining fields. Near this grave-yard, on the road-side, may be seen
the *well of St. Fintan*, from which a stream of clear water flows. At
present, there are no remains of an old building traceable, in the last
described cemetery. Nor are any ancient monuments to be found at

Clonenagh, with the exception of a small stone cross, evidently not occupying its former position. It was placed at the head of a recently made grave, in the month of August, 1856, when I last visited this interesting locality, which might well induce a train of reflections, contained in these following lines of the Rev. Matthew West, curate of St. Mary's Church, Donnybrook, during a portion of the last century:

" What objects here, but pensive thought inspire ?
What sounds, but seem mortality to mourn?
The ivy-mantled arch, the moss-clad spire,
The column from the mould'ring basis torn,
The bat slow wheeling through yon evening sky,
The beetle's solemn hum, and owl's foreboding cry !"

[3] According to a tradition of the place, as given by an intelligent peasant of this neighbourhood, St. Fintan was born near Maryborough, in the Queen's county. He mentioned the name of a townland, which has now escaped my memory; but I recollect he said this natal place was within a mile of the shire town of the Queen's county, and in a direction extending towards Clonenagh. The same informant stated, that according to tradition, St. Fintan first inhabited Cremogue, a place about three miles distant from Clonenagh. This saint was obliged to leave the former and take up his residence at the latter place. It is said, that when his monks had brought the building materials to both of these sites, the churches of Cremogue and Clonenagh were severally built, in the course of one night—although at different intervals. At a very early age, the writer recollects having had his attention attracted to an old causeway, which debouched, near Clonenagh, on the main road between Maryborough and Mountrath. This extended across a bog, in the direction of Cremogue, and appeared to have been constructed on the principle of our modern macadamized roads—many stones used, however, were of enormous size, and such as are generally employed for building purposes. This causeway was called "St. Fintan's road," and its construction is said to have been instantaneous, and of miraculous origin. The wild and romantic character of this legend impressed itself vividly on the writer's imagination at that time. The old road of St. Fintan has now in a great measure disappeared, and merged into a tolerably

4*

good bog-road of more recent construction. A bog-drain runs in a parallel direction. Between this drain and the modern road, that ancient causeway of St. Fintan may yet be traced. The writer was enabled to travel near and over the latter, during his short tour from Clonenagh to Cremogue. The "well of St. Fintan" does not at present occupy its original site. Persons were accustomed to resort to it for the cure of various diseases, leaving humble votive offerings, to mark their sense of the sanitary favours there received. Its Protestant landed proprietor contrived to divert the spring from his field to the road-side, and thus relieve his lands from a constant influx of those he deemed troublesome and superstitious visitants. Such was an account received by the writer, on occasion of a visit to the spot, already alluded to, when he was shown a sycamore tree, on the side of the public road and opposite the "well of St. Fintan." Within two or three cavities in the trunk of this tree, and at a considerable elevation from the ground, a small quantity of water was to be found. It is said that this water was first discovered, when the outrage offered to the feelings of the Catholics living near the neighbourhood had been committed, in this successful effort to divert the holy well from its original site. During the greatest heats of summer or the coldest days of winter, this water is to be found undiminished in quantity and unfrozen. Its production is regarded as miraculous, and as indicative of the displeasure of St. Fintan, for what the peasantry are pleased to consider a desecration of his well, at which perhaps,

"In the sylvan solitude, or lonely mountain cave,
Beside it passed the hermit's life, as stainless as its wave,"

to quote the beautiful lines of a native poet, J. D. Ffraser, in his verses on the Holy Wells of Ireland. In consequence of prevailing tradition, the veneration entertained even yet for the "well of St. Fintan" has been more universally transferred or extended to this tree in question, the branches of which are covered with scraps of ribbon, linen, &c., as votive offerings. Its trunk and boughs exhibit marks of the footsteps of devout or curious visitants, who are obliged to climb some distance, in order to procure water, contained in the higher cavity. From a peculiar formation of the tree, this ascent is by no means difficult or dangerous. Those cavities, in which the water lies, are really curious, and by no means of artificial construction. It need scarcely be observed, that this water is not of a pure quality, although perfectly clear. Hence it is not drunk, but is only used for lotions. From the person, who pointed out this interesting object, the writer also learned, that according to local tradition, those waters, contained in the original "well of St. Fintan," on being diverted from their first site, were in great part transferred immediately to Cremogue, about three miles distant. On their way thither, wherever a drop of those waters fell, a spring or pool was produced on the instant. The origin of this deposit, in the road-side tree, was thus accounted for; and reference was made to many other places, where water existed, on a direct line, from the "well of St. Fintan," at Clonenagh, to a spring denominated from him in like manner, near the old church and grave-yard of Cremogue. This water in the "well of St. Fintan," at Cremogue, is pure and very clear. The bottom of its spring contains a number of small white pebbles, which are held in great request, by the neighbouring peasants. It is believed, that the retaining of these will be a preservative against death, by any kind of untoward accident; and hence, those, who are about emigrating to distant countries, or engaging in any sort of dangerous enterprize, are anxious to secure possession of one of them, to be worn as an amulet on the person. Even, it has been known, that perfect strangers to this part of the country have in some instances sent commissions from the East and West Indies, from America and Australia, to procure these pebbles of Cremogue, having heard of their imputed efficacy, from exiled natives of this place. A peasant of its neighbourhood remarked, in hearing of the writer, that some ash trees, which grew near Cremogue well, having been cut down, by the farmer to whom they belonged; this man was afterwards reduced, within a very short period, to great indigence from a state of comparative affluence. This account, however, and many other particulars, regarded as miraculous by the country people, may well be assigned to natural causes. There is no tomb of great antiquity in the grave-yard at Cremogue. A ruined church, which is of ancient origin, may be seen; but it is evident, from present appearances, that it has undergone some modern renovations, and the belfry attached is not a building referable to any very remote date. Perhaps, like the old church of Clonenagh, Cremogue had been fitted up for Protestant services, at a comparatively late period. Many of the peasantry, to the present day, when passing the "well of St. Fintan," at Clonenagh, take off their hats, and make a sign of the cross on their foreheads—a custom which the writer had an opportunity of witnessing. The "well of St. Fintan" at Cremogue is also held in much veneration, by the country people. But neither the published Life of St. Fintan, as given in Colgan's *Acta Sanctorum Hiberniæ*, nor the etymological meaning of the word, would induce a supposition, that this place had any immediate connexion with our saint. The nomenclature, which means "Mogue's earth," would seem rather to refer to a saint bearing the name of Mogue; and a very remarkable abbot, called Mogue—the patron of Timahoe—might also have been the founder of a religious establishment, at Cremogue.

No. XXIII.

A Legend of the Cove of Cork.

FEAR DARRIG.

Spite the First.

THE ARGUMENT.

Fear Darrig from the country hies,
Cork's citizens to see,
Then moves where Spike so grimly lies,
Below the river Lee.

A glimpse of Cove Harbour.

Wide heave the fretting waters, land-locked round,
Those beauteous shores of Cove, [1] that circling bound
Scenes, fair as any distant lands may boast,
Spread o'er the swelling hills, which skirt that coast,
Where pointing to azure skies,
A thousand masts arise,
And swelling sails spread out
Flit gay about
The spit of Haulbowline, [2]
Near Rocky Island with its powder-mine. [8]
Skilled yachtmen cleave the harbour's chafing floods
By towers and brilliant lights,
Oft scudding tow'rds Rostellan's bowery woods, [4]
Cove and its overhanging heights,

Or through that strait, where frowning bide,
On either side,
Forts Camden and Carlisle, [5] high o'er the cliff-closed tide.

A paternal government's asylum for the treatment of incurables.

Spike Island [6] dépôt shell-proof stood
Above the flood,
In its full pride of station,
A fortress key
Below the Lee,
With cannoneers to guard
Its motley convict population;
Where hornwork bank and ravelin
Keep watch and ward
'Gainst strangers coming in,
Or natives moving out, to change their situation.

Fear Darrig sets out on his rambles.

Once on a time, the frisky Crimson Sprite,
Ycleped Fear Darrig, [7]
Took his journey during night,
From the old castle of Carrig, [8]
To a patrician house in the " beautiful city,"
Where unseen by mortal eyes, he chanted many a merry
ditty,
Which to the listening ear
Sounded musically clear,
Like notes of Brendan's heaven-sent bird, with warbling
strain,
Thrilling the ravished soul in Clonfert's ancient fane. [9]

Changes his domicile.

Strange clattering,
Within the servants' hall,
And chattering,
At midnight hour, were heard by all,
Until this free-and-easy liver
In search of other quarters rambled down the river,
Where the Royal Artillery
Manned bastions and casements of the Lee.

Enters the Artillery Barracks.

Through a massive well-barred gate
Fear Darrig passed the sentry,
At Spike Island barrack-yard ;
Silent the place, the time was late,
When pacing near its entry,
The carbineer on guard
.Heard some one gliding stealthily along,
And trolling out in accents strange a mellow Irish song. [10]

Challenged by the sentry.

The soldier looked above, below, around,
Nothing saw, yet heard the sound,
And tremulous with fear
Cried, " Stand !—who goes there ?"

Declares his intentions.

" A friend !" responded Darrig.
"Advance, friend ! and give the countersign !"

" I lately," said the sprite, " came from Carrig.
But when in Cork, I could not spare much time,
Or call for a governor's order :
Yet spite of gun or sword,
Without the pass-word,
Or even having license from its warder,
I mean to take possession of your castle.
As serves the future whim,
I will begin
To sport or serve within [11]
Chambers, kitchen, mess-rooms, when feasts abound and
wassail."

The alarm.

Bang went the signal gun ;
Out turned the night-watch guard ;
But the unseen sprite of fun
Passed through the barrack-yard ;
Whilst lanterns flashing bright
'Mid the dim, uncertain light,
And hoarse excited cries
Caused the garrison to rise,
As if some invading foe
Shot and shell began to throw.
But vain the search, though strangely told and true
The sentry narrated his tale ;
From slumbers aroused, the soldiers find no clue
Any foeman to assail ;
Yet wondering much, if mortal dare intrude,
Within their lines at that still hour of rest and solitude.

Fytte the Second.

THE ARGUMENT.

Tells how in Royal Barrack lines
Amongst th' Artillery ranks,
A mischief-loving genius shines,
In sport, whim, quips and cranks.

Fear Darrig's practical jokes.

Settled in this new home
The Crimson Man would roam
Like Jack the Giant Queller,
Making such tremendous rout
From garret down to cellar
Chattels were moved about.
All the kitchen wenches
Often heard and sometimes saw him vaulting over benches
Then would he sudden disappear
Like the Mantis of Brazil, [12]
Crowing as the plum'd chanticleer,
When morn's light began to steal.
Next upon the bells,
He rang incessant peals,
Calling maids or butlers up in haste
Idly to assist in halls or at the feast,
And when told there was no need,
For their presence or such speed,
They return back again to former quarters,
Enraged and wildly looking, like tameless Turks or Tartars.

Enforces discipline.

Daily growing bolder,
He often cuffed some tipsy, straggling soldier,
When late entering through the door :
Quick as thought
Lowly was the hero brought
And laid sprawling on the floor.
When this noisy Crimson Elfin railed
The stoutest warrior quailed.
He promptly bound all rioters to order
Within the narrow limits of their island border.

His prowess as a sportsman.

Locks he wrenched from bolted doors,
And opened military stores,
Then with shot and powder planteously supplied,
Like a fowler in the field
Could Fear Darrig skilful wield
His detonating weapon pointed fairly o'er the tide,
Till the well-directed shot
From sky had downward brought
The gory plumag'd gulls, which o'er the ocean flew ;
And oft his loaded gun
Pealed round the shores, where wheeled the screaming mew.
Then back again, alive to mirth and fun,
Through the racket courts,
Joining in their sports,
Many a stroke and ace
He marred with eager race,

Scoring high for officers he loved,
Or wresting game and stakes from others disapproved.

Disarranges the toilet-tables.

Again the meddling Crimson Sprite,
As officers had leave of absence day or night,
Would frequent hide their dressing cases,
When starting for Regattas, Hunting-meets or Races,
And their wardrobes disarranged;
He variously mislaid
Scents, bottles, perfumes, vases,
Macassar and pomade,
Though exquisites could little brook delay
Preparing for a ball or play.
To articles of taste no clue could they obtain,
Searching in vain
For Lavender or Eau de Cologne,
Tooth-powder, salves and honey-soap had flown,
He scatterred everywhere,
Hair-brushes, razors, toilet-ware.

His dinner-table delinquencies.

When plates were laid for dinner,
The mischief-loving sinner
Through a medley of discourses
Sauces or gravies separated
From those dishes where they mated;
Reversed were soups and courses;
Glasses changed, decanters grouped with knives and forks;
Or when waiters nicked the champagne corks,

Off Darrig set them popping,
On many a flushed forehead hopping.
But ere the feast was over
Few mortals could discover
Where flesh, fish, desert or salads might be found :
And when the port or claret passed around,
'Mongst circulating bottles strangely jingled
Spoons, castors, ladles, cruets oft commingled.
The Crimson-covered Man was a Lord of Misrule ;
All heard his busy whirring o'er the board.
Many pupils may be thought to have studied in his school,
Whose dinners badly served to guests, few comforts ill
afford.

After-dinner practices.

With a round of toasts delivered from the chair,
Some vocalist would chant " God save the King!"
Fear Darrig perch'd on upper cornice tun'd that air
Of most disloyal import he could sing.
Yet much to men's surprise,
No figure met their eyes ;
And when the feasters rose
From their banquet-room the spirit instant goes
Whistling, whooping, singing,
Roaming through their chambers till the morning light,
And endlessly dinning
Riotous, noisy chorus sounds incessant through the
night :
These most effective rondeaus tend to keep
Eyes unclosed, when wearied inmates pine for sleep.

Annoys the litterateur.

An officer lived here,
Prose-writer, ode-maker, lyrist, sonneteer,
Who sent his courant stanzas to a favourite *Maga*,
With translations from Racine, Ariosto, Lope de Vega.
Oft Darrig spoiled an article
In monthly pages partible,
Turning an inky stream
O'er the white paper ream.
Our practised pamphleteer,
Once or twice in every year,
Penned an essay, learned, pointed and clear ;
But when the writer left his study-room,
The imp would often come,
And within his book-case
Works of reference displace ;
Turning titles upside-down,
He would cancel *memoranda*, or paging marks remove,
Whilst the Lieutenant in town
Spent long evenings in a thoughtless and merry mood at
Cove.

He wears out his welcome.

'Twere endless to relate the mimes he played,
While at Spike Island station ;
For various were the objects there mislaid,
Too long the tricksy imp his visit had delayed—
Most deemed it visitation :

5

Although in kindness then
He oftentimes did friendly turns for officers or men,
  All wished him absent from the River Lee,
Or farther banished to the shores of Egypt's and Arabia's
  Sea.

Fytte the Third.

THE ARGUMENT.

Guns, rations, knapsacks, safely stored,
  The Blue Artillery
And Crimson Spirit, placed on board,
  Cruise gaily out to sea.

The route from Spike Island.

At length, an order for removal came,
And transport ships were brought from o'er the main,
    When the Royal Artillery
    Packed baggage for the sea ;
     Then down the Cove of Cork
     Sailing at even,
     Through its wide haven,
  Whilst sailors chant and work,
Fear Darrig in the shrouds sang out, " Yo, heave, yo !"
  Or busy tugging at a rope,
    His clamourous voice would ope
With a " Heigh ho ! cheerily man, cheerily man, ho !"

A night at sea.

Freshly whilst the breezes blow,
  Amidst a dim grove of spars,
A hundred lamps are rocking slow ;
  Softly brilliant shine the stars,

Twinkling through the twilight
In myriads by midnight,
As the ships in gallant trim their swelling canvass show,
Whilst round the rocky headlands of a southern coast
they go.

The passage.

Another evening waned,
Braced was each main-stay,
Bearing on the lee-way;
The distant signals flamed,
From many tongues of land before.
Steering round the Wicklow shore,
By Bray's impending highland,
And doubling Dalkey Island,
Soon gleam'd Dunleary's light revolving;
Then rocking brightly on the lee
Shone Kish, a lone hermit of the sea.
Next the burners of Bailly thick mists dissolving
Gathering o'er the cliffs of Howth:
Poolbeg's stately guiding casements, nothing loath,
Dazzling *lumières* bewray,
To point the passing transports into Dublin Bay. [18]
Until within a port,
Near the Pigeon House Fort, [14]
And moored beside its quay,
The warriors in blue uniforms debark without delay.

Fear Darrig disappears from the stage.

Through their midst, the little crimson clothed sprite.
Of Lilliputian height,

Tramped along a causeway, wending towards the city,
        Seen by the flickering light,
And chanting forth with gleesome voice his favourite merry
    ditty.
            But whether at the bend,
            He rested in Ringsend ;
            Or bound for frolic took
            His course to Donnybrook ;
        As its fair was then in season,
·To many this latter might appear sufficient reason,
In accounting for the ramble of such a merry liver :
    Or if he travelled further up the river,
        Like a migrating stork, [15]
    Flying homeward on his way to Cork,
No further record of his journey ever
        Reached the Royal Artillery,
        From the Liffy or the Lee.

NOTES.

[1] I know of nothing, in the shape of a Guide Book, superior to Windale's *Historical and Descriptive Notices of the City of Cork and its vicinity, Gougaun-Barra, Glengariff and Killarney*. A new and an enlarged edition of this work has been published in Cork, by the Messrs. Bolster, in 1848. Doubtless, other hand-books may present whiter paper, clearer type, more artistic engravings; but the compressed information and mode of imparting it are alone peculiar to the work of this accomplished local antiquary. The stranger will well find his way under such a *cicerone* to those varied points of interest in the "beautiful City" of Cork, the outlying town of Cove, and its magnificent harbour, where ships of any burden may ride in safety, at

every state of the tide. In 1786, Cove was only an insignificant village, consisting of some few huts, tenanted by fishermen and tide-waiters. The salubrity of its air, the fine scenery surrounding it, and the peculiar facilities afforded by railroad and river steamers for reaching Cork city, at convenient intervals, cause it to be much frequented and a favourite place for residence. Its houses and streets for the most part, line the beach, under eminences to their rear; but beautiful villa residences, with superb views, spread around it in every direction. Its present population exceeds 10,000 inhabitants.

[2] Hawlbowline is a *dépot* for naval and military stores, immediately opposite the town of Cove. It is said to have derived its name from the circumstance, that a chain or cable, at one time, had been drawn from it to Whitepoint across the channel. This chain was fastened to the bow of a vessel, and was hauled in therefrom every night, to prevent vessels passing up the river after dark. It was formerly called *Inis Sinneach*, or "Fox Island." The *Spit* sand-bank extends from it in an eastern direction.

[3] It contains at the present time about 200 tons of gunpowder In the beginning of last century, it was called Creagh Island.

[4] Rostellan Castle and its finely wooded demesne close the eastern extremity of Cove Harbour.

[5] These batteries occupy opposite sides of the entrance to Cove Harbour from the sea. Some of the best conducted convicts, drafted from Spike Island, are allowed special immunities there under improved prison discipline at the present time.

[6] Formerly called *Innyspynge* or *Inyspyk* forms a very prominent object in Cove harbour. Whether the name be derived from a former possessor, named John Pyke who obtained a grant of it in 1427, or whether the epithet *spic* or *spice*, an acute-pointed instrument had been applied to the sharp projection that formerly distinguished it more than at present, may be fairly questioned. A number of convicts are here usually employed in strengthening the fortifications, around Westmoreland Fort. They are kept under the *surveillence* of a strong guard belonging to the engineer department. A considerable Artillery force is usually distributed amongst the cantonments around the magnificent Harbour of Cove.

[7] The ꝼeaꞃ ꝺeaꞃᵹ, pronounced *Fear Darrig*, which means the Crimson or Red Man, a merry sprite of the fairy tribe, loves ingenious mischief, tricks and whimsical pranks. He appears in many of his properties to claim kindred with Puck the Fairy, Robin Goodfellow, the Scotch Brownie or Red Cap, and the German Kobold. The Fear Darrig love tidiness and neatness amongst mortals. They are supposed to haunt particular houses, especially in the south of Ireland. It is also said, they have a peculiar desire to occupy military quarters and accommodate themselves to the habits of soldiers. Their appearance betokens good luck. The melodious flexibility of the *Fear Dearg's* voice is compared by Irish story-tellers to the sound of the waves, to the music of angels, and to the warbling of birds. He is always dressed in crimson, when seen by mortals. The usual Irish address of those holding intercourse with him is, *Na dean fochmoid fáinn*, which means in English, "do not mock us!" He is known for his amusement to transform mortals into the most ridiculous shapes for a while, but they afterwards reassume their natural appearance. Sometimes, he is found clinging to or climbing amongst the thick masses of ivy, that surmount the parapets of many old castles.

[8] Within the parish of Carrigleamleary, in the barony of Fermoy, county of Cork, the ruins of Carrig Castle are seen on the summit of a rock which hangs over the Blackwater river. It lies within the beautiful demesne of Carrig Park, and on the northern bank of

> "Swift Awnduff, which of the English man
>   Is cal'de Blacke-water ;"

and all the scenery, surrounding this locality, is delightfully varied and highly picturesque in character.

[9] On a certain occasion, as is related in an old MS. of the Royal Irish Academy, whilst St. Brendan was in his church at Clonfert, a bird came from Paradise into his church, and perched over the altar. By striking a wing with his bill, this bird produced most enchanting melody. After this incident, all earthly music seemed so inharmonious to the saint, that he was obliged to keep his ears stopped with wax, lest the songs of this world might grate too harshly on his sense of hearing.

[10] The *Fear Dearg* is generally invisible, but he is heard chattering, singing and laughing, about the house, both by day and by night. He changes his voice like a ventriloquist. The tricks which he practises are simply mischievous, and usually end in a pleasant and ridiculous manner. The lines of Boileau may be considered peculiarly applicable to his habits:

" Il veut être folâtre, évaporé, plaisant :
 Il s'est fait de sa joie une loi nécessaire,
 Et ne déplaît enfin que pour vouloir trop plaire."

He is sometimes found very obliging, by doing household work for a favourite family, and often whilst its members are asleep. His visits and mode of departure are generally whimsical. I have been told a story, relating to the tolerably well preserved Castle of Tinnakill, near the banks of the River Barrow, within a few miles of Portarlington. Some time during the last century, this old embattled keep had been tenanted by a popular widow lady, called Poll Jones. Every night, when the family retired to rest, *Fear Dearg* used to visit the castle, and wind or spin immense quantities of woollen thread or yarn before daylight, when he vanished. The good mistress of the castle, thinking the winter nights too cold for the friendly sprite, remarked before retiring to bed, on one particular occasion, that she would leave his best silk cloak to warm the little house fairy. The sprite alluded to happened to overhear this remark, and most unaccountably felt huffed at the kindness intended him. He called out in a shrill voice: "No, I'll never spin or reel for Poll Jones, with silk on my elbows!" That was his parting declaration, for he never afterwards resumed his thrifty pursuits in the old castle. The poet Wordsworth has written a song for the Spinning Wheel, which is founded on a belief, prevalent among those inhabiting the pastoral vales of Westmoreland. It seems almost coincident with the circumstances of this story :

" Swiftly turn the murmuring wheel !
  Night has brought the welcome hour,
 When the weary fingers feel
  Help, as if from fairy power ;
 Dewy night o'ershades the ground,
 Turn the swift wheel round and round !"

[11] The Brownie of Scotland is a house working fairy. If kindly fed and treated, he would do a great deal of useful work. Of this spirit King James I. speaks in his *Dæmonology*, p. 127, as a rough man that haunts dwellings without perpetrating any evil, " but doing as it were necessarie turnes up and downe the house." The sage monarch tells us that " some were so blinded as to believe that their house was all the sonsier, as they called it, that such spirits resorted there." Milton, in his agreeable poem L'Allegro, alludes to this sprite and to the current cottage tales of his day, when the rustic

> "Tells how the drudging goblin sweat
> To earn his cream-bowl duly set,
> When in one night, ere glimpse of morn,
> His shadowy flail had thresh'd the corn,
> That ten day-labourers could not end ;
> Then lies him down the lubber fiend,
> And, stretch'd out all the chimney's length,
> Basks at the fire his hairy strength ;
> And crop-full out of door he flings,
> Ere the first cock his matin rings."

[12] The Mantis or Walking Leaf, so called from the elytra or cover of its wings assuming the appearance of plant foliage, in its various changes of hue, is a curious insect found in many southern districts of Europe, as also in Brazil. In this latter country, the negroes believe it endowed with some kind of preternatural instinct and that if asked, it will indicate, by its forefoot, the right course a traveller should take. This opinion was probably derived from the Europeans who settled in that country ; as a similar notion is known to prevail on the Continent of Europe. This insect is often called the Invisible, because he is supposed to be gifted with power to escape or disappear at any moment from his enemy. He often reposes on his hind legs, and in this position resembles a diminutive human being. From his grave and methodical motions or eccentric appearance, he i supposed to be a species of diviner, and hence has obtained the name Mantis or Soothsayer. His posture sometimes resembles that of a person, with elevated hands, in a state of absorbed contemplation. He is often noticed seemingly ravished with musical sounds, and apparently beating time to such harmony with a peculiar action of his

forefeet. He can live a long time without food, air or light, and has obtained the epithet " Immortal" from this wonderful tenacity of life

[13] There are few residents of Ireland's capital unacquainted with those fine effects produced by various artificial lights, streaming after sunset from the most distant points around the bay of Dublin, so justly celebrated for varied and exquisite views it affords. Besides the harbour lighthouses already named, populous suburban townships glow with numerous gas-lamps, which almost seem a necessity of modern street improvements.

[14] An Artillery Barracks and Magazine, at the southern entrance to Dublin Harbour.

[15] Storks are birds of passage which spend the summer in many countries of Europe. On the approach of winter, they depart southwards to Egypt, Ethiopia and other countries of Africa. About the middle of March, they usually fly northwards.

No. XXIV.

A Legend of St. Mullins.

———

THE WHITE GOBLIN.

ABOVE the Barrow's banks 'mid clustered thorns,
  A venerable chantry's walls are seen, [1]
And oft, 'tis said, a goblin lady warns
  Belated revellers. [2]   From her ivy screen
  Forth issuing through those boughs of darkest green,
She sails on air, in white and floating train,
  With icy clasp her arm will slowly lean,
And press with death's embrace the mounted swain,
For worse than plague the touch of her most fatal strain.

———————

NOTES.

[1] Allusion is here made to the interesting group of ruins, situated as described, in the barony of Lower St. Mullins, county of Carlow. They crown a beautiful and romantically placed ridge, rising over the Barrow's northern bank, yet at some little distance above its waters. Here, about the middle of the seventh century, St. Moling founded a monastic establishment. There is still extant an Irish poem, attributed to the celebrated Finn Mac Cool, and relating to the local features and future celebrity of Ros Broc, an ancient denomination for St. Mullins. Another name of this place had been Aghacainid; but it was afterwards called Tegh-Moling, after the name of its patron saint. He is said to have governed this house for many years—part of which were spent at Glendalough—until he was elevated to the See of Ferns, A.D. 691. We find him styled Arch-

bishop of that See. In the year 693, he induced Finnachta, monarch of Ireland, to exempt the Leinster province from a heavy tribute of oxen, with which it had long been burthened. Several prophecies have been attributed to St. Moling. He died on the 17th of June, A.D. 697. Soon after his death, the monastery was plundered by the Danes, A.D. 951, and it was destroyed by fire in 1158. Subsequently the Canons Regular of St. Augustine here founded an abbey, the ruins of which are yet visible. St. Mullins was the burial place of the Kavanaghs, kings of Leinster. Within the old walls may be seen a tomb erected over General Cloney, so celebrated in connection with the Rebellion of 1798.

[2] From the old grave-yard at this place, a lady clothed in a long and flowing white dress, has been sometimes known to proceed, when a solitary horseman may happen to be riding, at a late hour of the night, and along those roads, leading from St. Mullins, in various directions. She seats herself behind the rider, and grasps him around the waist. He becomes chilled with this cold embrace; and then, after riding with him for some time, the goblin lady disappears. Soon afterwards, the rider begins to decline in health, until death ensues, when it is thought the white lady claims him as a future tenant of that ancient burial ground, which she haunts.

L'Envoy.

—

If 'mid fond views of Erin's scenes
Bright Fancy weaves her changeful dreams,
And leads us from paths, cold and real,
Through sportive flights of the ideal ;
Through Homer's heroes, Maro's page,
With classic lore our minds engage,
Can fiction grave or brighter clime
Reveal more forms, gay or sublime ?
Like threads in clouded air that play,
And float unseen from thorn to spray,
Fine goss'mer lines of sparkling gold
They shine, when sunlight gilds the wold,
While shades roll off in wreath'd maze
Their tissues brighten to the rays ;
So lightest, loveliest shapes appear,
Strange tales of youth ripe age to cheer,
Reviving themes of earlier days—
The Fairy Realms and Legend Lays.
Once more ecstatic thought will spring
To wizard worlds, on aerial wing,
Brushing with swifter sweep aside
Those darker ills our lives betide.

THE END.

JH